Beneath the Bonnet
A Collection of Regency Tales

Beneath the Bonnet
A Collection of Regency Tales

Featuring:
A Search for Refuge

Kristi Ann Hunter

Oholiab Creations
Georgia, United States

A Search for Refuge, © 2018 by Kristi Ann Hunter, originally published by Bethany House Publishers.

Saving Miss Caulfield originally published on Regency Reflections blog, 2015

Three O'Clock in Portman Square, originally published in Splickety magazine, November 2017

The Heir Next Door originally published in Spark magazine, 2022

Published by Oholiab Creations, LLC

www.kristiannhunter.com

No part of this publication may be reproduced, stored in a retrieval system, or transmitted in any form or by any means—for example, electronic, photocopy, recording—without the prior written permission of the publisher. The only exception is brief quotations in printed reviews.

ISBN 978-1-959589-12-9

This is a work of fiction. Names, characters, incidents, and dialogues are products of the author's imagination and are not to be construed as real. Any resemblance to actual events or persons, living or dead, is entirely coincidental.

Scripture quotations are from the King James Version of the Bible.

Cover design by Angie Fisher at WTX Labs

Author's Notes

Thank you for picking up Beneath the Bonnet: A Collection of Regency Tales.

This collection features A Search for Refuge, originally published as a promotional eBook to open the Haven Manor series. Looking for the eBook? You can still get it free wherever you purchase eBooks.

Following A Search for Refuge you'll be able to enjoy three short stories. Two are pieces of flash fiction originally published with Splickety and Spark magazines. Saving Miss Caulfield is a piece I wrote for a blog prior to my first published stories.

Now all of these previously digitally available stories can sit on your bookshelf. Enjoy!

A Search for Refuge

One

MARLBOROUGH, ENGLAND, 1804

Margaretta had used the word *desperate* many times in her life, but she'd never truly known the meaning until she stood in the open door of a mail coach, clutching an eight-month-old letter and praying that someone in this minuscule market town would know where the writer had gone when she moved on.

And that Margaretta could find that writer before Samuel Albany found her.

Because that writer was Margaretta's last hope. And hope was something Margaretta desperately needed to find. In the truest sense of the word.

"Are you getting out here, miss?"

Margaretta forced her gaze away from the broad stone-cobbled street lined with red-bricked buildings and porticoed storefronts. The man holding the door and growing justifiably impatient wore the red coat of the English mail service and thick layer of travel dust. To him, Margaretta likely appeared a woman without a care in the world compared to his current discomfort.

If he knew she was running for her life, would he still think that?

Not that it mattered. His opinion couldn't matter. No one's could. Margaretta knew the truth, knew what decisions she would be willing to live with, and that was all that could be allowed to matter.

"Yes, I'm getting off." She shoved the letter into the pocket of her bright yellow cloak and wrapped her hand around the worn leather handle of her valise. The heavy bag bumped against her knee as she climbed down, threatening to toss her on top of the dirty mail worker and flatten his nose even more. She jumped instead, jarring her knees as her walking boots hit the ground. It was an unladylike exit from the vehicle to say the least, but far better than landing on the ground on her backside.

Blowing a hard breath out between pursed lips, Margaretta stepped to the side and set her valise at her feet. She adjusted the hood of her cloak so that it shadowed her face. Yes, it made it difficult to see around her, but it also kept people from seeing her. She'd much rather people remember the enormous hood of a ridiculous bright yellow cloak than her face. As a woman traveling alone on the stage, people were going to look at her. It was either wear something memorable and distracting or cover herself in the somber colors of mourning, which she wasn't willing to do. That would be like admitting defeat before she'd even begun.

Lifting her valise, she turned her head to survey the town with a critical eye. It was charming, with a considerable openness she'd never experienced in London, but she didn't have the luxury of standing around, pondering the benefits of fresh air and space. Her time was limited, her funds even more so. If she was going to solve her problems before both of those commodities ran out, she was going to have to be smart. And while she'd tried very hard to always be prudent and practical, clever had never been required of her.

She slid a hand into her pocket and curled it around the already wrinkled paper. Her friend Katherine had always been clever, though, and Margaretta was counting on being able to follow her friend's clever path to make sure everything turned out as it should and everyone stayed safe for at least the next few months.

Hopefully Katherine hadn't been so clever that Margaretta's efforts were entirely futile. This letter was the last connection Margaretta had to her friend, and it held pitifully little information.

Exhaustion crowded Margaretta's mind. She'd been traveling for three days straight, taking mail coach after mail coach on a wide route around London to avoid anyone who might be looking for her. As long as everyone thought her safely tucked away in Margate, sea-bathing with Mrs. Hollybroke and her daughters, she would have time. Time to hide, time to come up with a plan, time to accomplish the impossible task of finding Katherine. Since complete disappearance seemed to be part of Katherine's solution, Margaretta could only hope her letter was the start of a small trail of breadcrumbs.

So the questions was, if Margaretta wanted to find someone who didn't particularly want to be found—where would she start?

Her stomach grumbled and clenched, reminding her that the meat pie she'd consumed at a roadside inn for breakfast had been eaten a very long time ago.

She wasn't going to do anyone any good, particularly not herself, if she collapsed from hunger and weariness in the middle of the street. Food and lodging first, then. Tomorrow she could start her search.

The large three-gabled inn to her right looked promising and comfortable. It also looked like it catered to the expensive tastes of those traveling from London on the stagecoaches. Not only would staying there make her purse dwindle faster than she'd like, it would also put her at risk of running into someone she knew. She couldn't have anyone going back to London with the news that Margaretta was in Marlborough.

So she started walking. Away from the inn and the delightful smells drifting out of it. Away from the coach and the people with whom she'd spent the past several hours sharing a tiny space.

Away from everything she was familiar with.

Travel was something she'd done a great deal of in her life. One didn't have a father in the business of saddles and harnesses without getting a chance or two to test out the leather creations. But never had she wandered alone, away from the areas populated with other travelers like herself.

A deep breath trembled its way into her tight lungs. She could do this. One foot in front of the other. Breathing in for two steps and out for two steps. Absorb the idyllic calm of the wide street that grew quieter the farther she got from the stable. Find something to focus on and just keep moving until a solution presented itself. It was a scary prospect that made her normally pragmatic self shake in her boots, but for the past month and a half it had served her well. Pick a point and move toward it.

Farther down the street, a woman swept the pavement in front of a store. The sign simply read *Lancaster's*, but the array of bundled herbs hanging in the window and the barrels of food beneath indicated the store was likely a grocer. Margaretta's stomach grumbled again. It wouldn't be a gourmet meal, but if she could patch together a meal of fruit and cheese and perhaps other foods not requiring much preparation, she'd spend less than half of what she'd have to spend in an inn's public room.

It was as good as any other option she had at the moment. Her lips flattened into a line of determination as she gathered her strength together and moved toward the grocer, trying to ignore the nervous fear that made her want to glance over her shoulder to see if anyone was following her.

Nash Banfield stepped away from the door to his office and followed the woman down the street.

Given the location of his office just off Marlborough's central street, he'd seen many a person disembark from a variety of carriages. Normally he paid them only mild attention, but the brightness of this woman's cloak had been impossible to miss as she paused in the door of the carriage, a spot of sunshine framed by faded, dusty paint and the thin grey clouds that covered the sky.

Clouds that made it strange that she took time to pull the enormous hood over her head, shielding her dark hair and pale skin from view.

No one had joined her, and she'd claimed none of the trunks and bags being removed from the top of the carriage. Instead she'd taken her lone leather valise and walked with firm strides away from the coach, the inn, and all of the people.

Nash had been a solicitor for many years, and he'd rarely seen anything good come from someone traveling alone, traveling light, and hiding her face.

He'd seen that face for only a few moments before the hood had cast the strong brows and full mouth into deep shadow. From this distance, he couldn't make out the emotion riding her features, but there had been little doubt of the strength with which she felt it. It was evident in the square of her shoulders, the press of her lips, the determination in her pace.

In Nash's experience, strong emotion of any kind had the potential to turn dangerous.

Mr. Tucker, a well-dressed man who owned one of the local cheese factories, passed her, tipping his hat as he went.

The woman didn't acknowledge him, and instead turned away to cross the street. The folds of her yellow cloak swirled around her, revealing a dress of deep blue underneath it.

Nash pressed his lips into a flat line as he clasped his hands together at his lower back and waited, watching to see where she was going. It wasn't that a stranger in town was anything new. Many people dressed as fine as she and considerably finer came through town, viewing it as a humble and rustic resting point between London and Bath.

Most of those people didn't take the mail coach, though.

In a few days, the town would be bursting with people—strangers and locals alike. When the weekly market came to town, Marlborough would explode with people. The wide cobblestoned street would be filled to capacity, if not beyond it, and noise would echo from the tall roofs and narrow side alleys. But right now, the town was quiet.

It was a small community; only two parishes divided the town, and the people who roamed the streets and did their business during the week were close. They'd surrounded Nash after the death of his sister, helped him heal from the final loss of the last person he had held so dear, kept him from retreating into a dark and consuming melancholy that he feared would come for him.

They'd become his family.

Nash's hands dropped to his side, and his natural inquisitive curiosity shifted toward grave concern as it became evident that the woman was walking straight for Mrs. Lancaster's store. The older woman had kept the business after the death of her husband, continuing to provide a place for Marlborough's residents to buy food, spices, and a variety of other items during the week without waiting for the crush of Saturday's market. But the woman was generous to a fault, particularly to young women. She'd befriended many of the ladies who worked in the local poorhouses and replaced more than one little girl's wooden graces hoop without asking for a penny in return.

When Mr. Lancaster had gotten sick, he'd asked Nash to promise to look after his wife. That had been nearly five years ago, but it hadn't taken long for Nash to learn that watching over Mrs. Lancaster wasn't easy, considering the fact that the woman never did anything in a way that could remotely be considered normal. Nash dreaded the day someone took advantage of the old widow's kindness.

Someone like a woman who got off a stage and headed straight for the grocer. Perhaps she knew she'd be able to trade a sad story for gain.

He pushed off from the wall and strolled down the street. The people of Marlborough had saved him eight years ago. This town was the only family he had left. He was ready to protect it if necessary.

Margaretta's eyes widened as she took in the shelves and barrels of foodstuffs, herbs, and a myriad of other things she'd have never thought to find in a grocer. Did they have stores like this in London? She'd never really done the shopping in London, at least not for food. Ribbons and hats and gloves were interesting, but they didn't provide the same visual texture and smells as a room full of culinary potential.

Everywhere she looked she saw something else, something she wanted to remember next time she sat with the housekeeper to dither over the menu, to make slight adjustments in the planned dishes and anticipate how excited her father would be to have something new on the table that evening.

Of course, it would be a long time before she could return to their townhouse in London and while away the morning with a menu and her imagination. Right now, she was more interested in the baskets of late-season apples and nectarines and was giving serious consideration to eating them in a back alley despite the fact that they were raw. She was simply too hungry to care and didn't have a means to cook them anyway.

The woman she'd passed as she entered hummed as she followed Margaretta inside and stored her broom in a nook near the door. The tune was vaguely familiar. A song she'd heard in church, perhaps? It was not a tune that lent itself to dancing so it couldn't have been from a ballroom.

Margaretta's mouth watered as her senses adjusted to the quiet of the grocer after the noise of the traveling coach. She could smell cheese and bread in addition to the various herbs and spices that filled more shelves. It was a welcome change from horses and the unwashed bodies of travelers. The room was dim, forcing her to push her hood back, so she kept her back to the door as the woman approached.

"Well, now, don't get many customers fresh off the stage. What can I get you?" The woman rounded the counter. She was spry, though her right foot drug a bit behind her as she walked. Age rested comfortably on her round face, framed by a few gray-streaked brown curls escaping from the cap on her head.

"Two of each of these, please." Margaretta indicated the fruit baskets as she set her bag on the floor in front of her feet, making sure to drape the edge of her cloak over it. "Perhaps a bit of cheese and a small loaf of that bread."

The lady nodded and began bundling Margaretta's choices in a piece of brown paper while she talked. "This is the best bread in the county, but don't tell Mr. Abbot at the bakery down the street. Still irks him that I sell loaves for Cecily White in my store, but there's nothing he can do about it. You're lucky she was late bringing them in today. I usually sell out by noon."

Margaretta carefully counted coins from her reticule. She couldn't help but smile as the woman prattled on, but her expression turned into an embarrassed frown when her stomach rumbled a loud protest at the delay of food.

Without pausing her sentence, the woman tore off a chunk of the bread and handed it to Margaretta before wrapping the rest of the loaf in the parcel. "Now if you're wanting biscuits, I'll send you down to Mr. Abbot. He sells the best, though his daughter is the one what actually makes them. But we all pretend his wife does it, even though she struggles to even roll out a pie crust. What business that woman had marrying a baker is beyond me."

The woman looked up with a wink. "Oh, hello there, Mr. Banfield. What brings you by today?"

Her eyes cut to Margaretta as she spoke, giving the distinct impression that the older woman believed her customer had been the lure for the gentleman's visit instead of the vast array of foodstuffs.

Margaretta tried to look at the newcomer out of the corner of her eye. All she could see as he doffed his top hat was a mass of dark hair and a simple brown single-caped great coat.

"Good afternoon, Mrs. Lancaster. I'm afraid I ran out of peppermints." He stopped next to Margaretta at the counter.

Mrs. Lancaster gave a half laugh. "Well, come on back here and get them, then. You know where they are since you just purchased a tin two days ago."

The man stepped behind the counter and crossed behind the old shopkeeper. His bright blue eyes focused on Margaretta as he passed, and she tried not to stare back, but was still able to make out a straight, thin nose and strong chin.

"Have you met this lovely young lady yet?" Mrs. Lancaster asked as she took Margaretta's money.

Mr. Banfield turned, a small tin in his hand and a half smile on his lips. "No, I'm afraid I haven't had the pleasure."

"Me either." The woman grinned at him, her face settling into the lines of a smile with comfortable ease, proving that all the wrinkles in her face weren't put there by age. "We can indulge ourselves together, then, shall we?"

Margaretta swallowed two nibbles of bread down hard as the woman's wide smile beamed in her direction. She wanted to take her food and run, to hold on to her privacy and anonymity, but she was going to have to talk to people if she wanted to find Katherine, and it would be much less suspicious if she talked to everyone. So she did her best to smile back.

"I'm Mrs. Lancaster, dearie. And this here is one of our local solicitors, Mr. Banfield. Seeing as you're new in town, we're probably the best two people to know. I know all the best places to get into trouble, and he knows how to get you out of it."

Her cackling laugh sounded considerably younger than she appeared, with a lilt to it that could take the edge off of any number of potentially offensive statements.

Margaretta had no idea what to say to that and the discomfort caused the heat of a blush to ride high across her cheekbones.

Mr. Banfield stepped forward, his attention finally diverted from Margaretta to the old woman. His smile was indulgent, and it was obvious he cared for the woman. "Mrs. Lancaster, the only time you get into trouble is when you attempt to help others get out of it."

His gaze swung from Mrs. Lancaster to Margaretta, losing the air of loving indulgence as the smile fell into a flat line, and he braced his feet to confront her.

Margaretta straightened her shoulders and stuck her nose in the air, not caring if it made her look haughty. She'd done nothing to earn this man's derision and held his gaze while she answered the shopkeeper in order to prove it. "How nice to meet you, Mrs. Lancaster. I am Mi—" She coughed to cover her hesitation. Who could she possibly say she was? Samuel was sure to be looking for a Mrs. Albany so she couldn't possibly give them her real name.

Being a *Miss* would be the easiest way to throw Samuel off should he come looking, but that would cause a host of other problems for Margaretta if she was still in town in a month or two. She coughed again to buy herself a bit of time and held up the chunk of bread with an apologetic smile.

"I'm Mrs.—" *Name! Name! She needed a name!* "Fortescue."

She nearly groaned. Using her maiden name was nearly as bad as admitting her married name was Albany. If Samuel came to Marlborough, he'd find her for sure.

Two

Nash slid the tin of peppermints into his coat pocket and reached beneath the counter to pull out Mrs. Lancaster's log book. He noted the price for the candy on his page of the ledger and then waited for it to dry. If he took twice the time necessary before closing the book, no one knew that but him.

That the woman was married surprised him, especially now that he could see her face up close. What sort of man let such a striking woman traipse about the country by herself on the mail stage? Wherever Mr. Fortescue was, he wasn't doing a very good job.

That, or Mrs. Fortescue was enough trouble to warrant more attention than Nash's mild concern and curiosity.

Mrs. Lancaster, unsurprisingly, didn't seem encumbered by any similar worries as she barreled on, talking as she did with everyone, whether friend or stranger. "And what brings you to Marlborough, Mrs. Fortescue? Have you come to stay for the market this weekend? You're in luck. I hear Mr. and Mrs. Blankenship will be setting up a stall. Finest pendants I've ever seen. Mr. Lancaster saved up for months and bought me a peacock brooch. One of my most treasured possessions."

Nash couldn't help the smile that quirked one side of his lips. Mrs. Lancaster always seemed to know just how much information to bait a hook with. He was fairly certain she knew everyone in town's personal business, which made Nash very glad that he didn't really have any. He handled the contracts, land agreements, and leases that people in the area needed, and he tried to help where he could, be a caring and friendly part of the town. But at night he went to his rooms alone. He didn't even employ a valet anymore, choosing instead to have one of the local laundresses see to the cleaning and mending of his clothing.

If he had to guess, though, he'd say that Mrs. Fortescue's amount of personal business more than made up for Nash's lack thereof.

The dark-haired woman clutched her paper-wrapped bundle a little tighter and flattened her lips in what was probably supposed to look like a smile, though her dark eyes remained flat and wary. "That sounds lovely, but I don't know if I will still be in town Saturday."

Nash slid the ledger back under the counter with a sigh of relief. If she was just passing through, his instincts were clamoring without reason. Dozens of troublesome people passed through Marlborough every day without causing a problem. Even Mrs. Lancaster couldn't help a person who wasn't there.

"Of course you will. No finer town in England than Marlborough. Now that you're here, you'll want to stay a while." Mrs. Lancaster nodded her head and poked a finger into the air as if her word was law and she expected everyone to obey it.

For the most part, people did. But in this case, Nash had a feeling they would all be better off if she didn't choose this particular lost soul to work her magic on. Was it the way Mrs. Fortescue was standing, guarding her bag and shielding herself from the world? The way she was very obviously hungry but didn't bear the look of someone who knew a lot about living life in such a condition? There was no doubt in Nash's mind that she was running, or at the very least, hiding. Not something Nash would willingly concern himself with, except that she'd looked so determined to bring her plight into Mrs. Lancaster's store.

He angled his head and smiled again at Mrs. Lancaster. "There is a world beyond Marlborough, you know, and some people do have obligations in it."

"I suppose that's true." The already short woman seemed to sink into herself a little bit, making her body appear as round as her face. "If everyone lived in Marlborough, we'd be a bit crowded."

A sigh of laughter sounded from Mrs. Fortescue and for the briefest moment her smile looked a little less forced. The moment was soon gone, and she settled back into a tense silence.

The desire to bring back that brief moment of lightness, to expand it until he was able to hear her laugh and see a true smile on her face hit Nash in the chest. Perhaps Mrs. Lancaster's inclination to save lost souls had worn off on him over the years. He tried to quash any such ambition with a dark frown. His allotment of personal charity was taken up by the members of this town, particularly those who had been taken advantage of and required his services at one point or another.

Mrs. Lancaster had never accepted his attempts to guard and rescue her though, and this moment didn't seem to be the exception. "Where are you off to, then?"

"I, um." The younger woman ran a finger along the seam of the folded paper on her package, revealing scratched and worn light brown gloves that were streaked with road dust. Too much damage and filth for a single day's travel from London.

She cleared her throat. "I'm not entirely sure."

Did she really not know where she was going or had she already reached her destination? Even if he assumed the best, that her seemingly pointed walk straight to Mrs. Lancaster had been coincidental, that didn't mean he could leave Mrs. Lancaster unprotected. The young woman was definitely on the run. What had she done?

Mrs. Lancaster slapped her hands on the counter. "Then there's no need to run off. You can stay here and see the market."

Nash cleared his throat. "Seems a strange part of the country for an exploratory pleasure jaunt. It's not like you'd sell many travel journals about the wonders of the wilds of Wiltshire."

Mrs. Fortescue took a deep breath and made that strange flattened attempt at a smile once more. No one was fooled. At least Nash wasn't. "I'm looking for—er, meeting someone."

Mrs. Lancaster clasped her hands to her chest, her round, lined face tightening into a broad smile. "Oh, people are ever so much more interesting than jewelry. Who are you looking for?"

Mrs. Fortescue darted a look at Nash before turning her dark eyes back to Mrs. Lancaster.

Nash frowned. Was she as wary of him as he was of her? Had she expected to find Mrs. Lancaster alone and vulnerable? Or was she truly a skittish woman in need of assistance? A dull throb took up residence at the base of Nash's neck.

The woman swallowed and straightened her shoulders once more, causing the voluminous yellow cloak to part, showing a simple dark blue gown underneath. He'd caught a glimpse of the skirt when she crossed the street earlier, but he hadn't expected the rest of the dress to be so plain. The neckline was only slightly rounded, not even requiring a chemisette to remain modest. Why would the owner of such a dress choose an eye-catching cloak?

"Just an old friend."

"May I see you to the location where you are meeting your friend?" Nash stepped from around the counter and bowed his head in Mrs. Fortescue's direction. It was the gentlemanly thing to do, offering to escort a lone woman, but it would also allow him to know who she was connected to in his little town.

The color that had begun to fade from her cheeks rushed back, perhaps even brighter than it had been before. She pressed her lips together before wetting them and giving a shaky smile. "Oh, no, that won't be necessary. I'm going to simply find a place to stay tonight and search for—er, meet them in the morning."

Nash's wariness eased, replaced by curiosity and concern, for both of the women in the room. Whoever this young woman was, subterfuge was not her normal style. The slips of speech were too prevalent. He supposed they could be intentional, but anyone with the ability to blush and stammer on command would have aimed for a much higher target than a small-town grocer. In fact, he was beginning to wonder if the unidentified emotion he'd seen earlier wasn't simply fear.

"There's a set of rooms above the shop." Mrs. Lancaster slid around the counter. "Mr. Banfield can take your bag upstairs if you'd like."

Nash swung around to look at Mrs. Lancaster. "You can't just take in a boarder without knowing anything about her," he said at the same time that Mrs. Fortescue piped up, "Oh, I couldn't possibly be such an intrusion."

Chocolate brown eyes narrowed as she frowned at Nash. "What are you implying, sir?"

Nash narrowed his gaze in return at the captivating woman he was more and more convinced by the minute was going to bring havoc into his neatly ordered life. Just because he'd absolved her of any nefarious intentions didn't mean he was ready to trust her. "I'm implying that she doesn't know you from Eve and therefore shouldn't give you free run of her property."

Mrs. Lancaster pushed her way in between them. "She's hardly the first young lady I've helped, Mr. Banfield. Why else do you think I'm always sweeping my steps when the mail comes through? I want to see who the good Lord brought to town for me to bless."

Nash sighed. "That's very noble of you, Mrs. Lancaster."

"Of course it is. That's what the Bible says to do after all, isn't it?" Mrs. Lancaster turned to Mrs. Fortescue. "Why don't you tell me about your friend? I might have helped her, too."

Mrs. Fortescue smiled at the older woman, a genuine smile even if the rest of the expression looked a little sad. "I'm afraid Katherine would have come through here quite a few months ago."

"Traveling alone, like you?" Nash asked, earning himself another frown from the woman. He snapped his teeth together with a click and turned his attention to look at whatever graced the nearest counter. He'd probably learn a lot more if he let Mrs. Lancaster do the talking. As long as he stayed nearby he could prevent the old woman from doing anything potentially detrimental to herself. But he couldn't stop himself from asking, "Where is your husband?"

Her eyebrows lifted. "Laid to rest in a field outside London. One can only hope he found his way to Heaven from there."

Margaretta lifted her chin and put every scrap of energy she had left into not dropping her gaze. Over and over again she reminded herself that she had nothing to be ashamed of. She'd done nothing wrong, and there was nothing this man could do to her.

Unless he knew her brother-in-law. Was there any chance Samuel would have enlisted the help of professional men around the country to look for her? It seemed a bit too organized and thorough for him, but Margaretta wasn't about to assume anything. It would be almost as bad if the man knew her father, but Mr. Banfield had had no reaction to the name Fortescue.

The next breath slid into her lungs with a little more ease than the last. For right now, at least, everything seemed to be as it should be.

She turned her best smile on the older woman, hoping her fear didn't show on her face. The chance that she could afford a set of rooms when she could barely afford to stay at an inn was slim, but here would be a much better place to hide if she could. "How much to use the rooms above?"

Mrs. Lancaster waved an arm about. "Dust and sweep the store and we'll consider it a trade. Not today, of course. You can start tomorrow."

"Mrs. Lancaster," the man nearly growled through gritted teeth.

The grocer frowned. "She just got off the stage, Mr. Banfield. Only a heartless termagant would put her to work right now, and we've already established I've more heart than you like."

Another bubble of mirth broke through Margaretta's tension, and she lifted a hand to cover the small chuckle that threatened to escape. But the stench of travel clinging to the glove reminded her exactly what her situation was and threw a wet blanket over any vestiges of humor. A smelly, wet, dust-covered blanket.

No one—not her father, not Samuel, not anyone she'd ever met in her entire life—would expect to find her sweeping floors in a simple shop with humble rooms above it. Mostly because she would never have dreamed of placing herself in such a situation, but right now, it was ideal. Her money would last longer, and maybe she'd have a chance to talk with Mrs. Lancaster alone. If anyone was going to remember Katherine, it was probably the nosy but endearing old woman.

Right now that sweet old woman was jabbing an elbow into Mr. Banfield's side. "Take her bag up and let her get settled. I've customers to tend to."

Mr. Banfield ran a hand along the back of his neck, stabbing his fingers through the hair at the back of his head. It was obviously not the first time today he'd done such a thing, either. Any style his hair had held today had been lost, ruined by too many encounters that called for similar gestures of frustration.

The man needed to learn to relax.

Not that Margaretta had any real claim to such ability at the moment, but he could hardly claim a dire predicament as the reason for his tension.

The last thing she wanted, though, was such a tense and suspicious man taking her bag. Custom-made for her by her leather-working father, there wasn't another satchel like it anywhere. Father was known for making the most exquisite saddles in

England, but the valise had been a special project just for her. She couldn't let Mr. Banfield get a close enough look at it to see the Fortescue Saddlery medallion on the clasp.

Margaretta cleared her throat as she scooped up her valise handle in one hand while the other clutched her bundle of food. "Please do not trouble yourself. The building is not very large, and there are only so many places the stairs can be located. I shall have no trouble seeing myself up."

His eyebrows lifted as his head jerked back a bit. "I'm sure you wouldn't. Nevertheless, I'd hate to disappoint Mrs. Lancaster. May I take your bag?"

Her grip tightened instinctively. She swallowed. If she were going to keep him from being too curious about her, she had to put him off guard. Until now, he'd been the one suspicious of her. What would he think if she turned the tables on him?

With more bravado than actual indignation, she stuck her nose into the air. "No, thank you. You've made no secret that you find my presence here unsettling. I'll not have you running off with my bag in an attempt to make me leave."

His hand went to his neck again, but this time it didn't push into his already disheveled hair as he dropped his gaze to stare in the vicinity of his toes and his shoulders slumped inward. A deep breath expanded his chest before he dropped his hand and straightened once more, a considerably softer look on his face. "My apologies. I assure I will keep all of my efforts to protect Mrs. Lancaster as honest as possible. I would never resort to anything so underhanded."

Not quite the apology she'd been hoping for, but she could work with it. "Nevertheless, I intend to hold on to my belongings for the time being as I have no one to protect *me* aside from myself."

A more heartbreakingly true sentence had never been uttered.

He tilted his head to the side and watched her for a moment before gesturing toward the back of the store. "The stairs are this way."

As they walked farther into the depths of the store, Margaretta marveled at the variety of goods around her. Since when did a grocer need a shelf displaying porcelain teacups and embroidered reticules?

"A sampling of wares from some of the people who will have stalls at Saturday's market," Mr. Banfield explained, noticing her gaze. "So many of the town's inhabitants spend the whole day selling that they've no time to peruse the other stalls. Mrs. Lancaster keeps a few select items on hand to sell during the week." He cleared his throat as he pushed open a door at the back of the shop that opened into a narrow alley. "I'm afraid the dusting and sweeping you agreed to is probably a bigger job than you thought."

Especially given that she'd never dusted or swept a thing in her life, unless one counted scooping a hand of cards off the table surface as dusting. She blinked a few times, hoping to clear her head from worry and the encroaching weariness so she could say something that convinced him she knew what she was doing. "I wouldn't expect anything less than a bit of hard work in exchange for the rooms."

He cleared his throat and looked up the stairs. "Your friend. I'd like to help you find her."

"You want to get rid of me that badly?"

She expected him to frown, but he didn't. He simply looked at her. "Perhaps, in my own way, I wish to help those who find themselves in a basket as much as Mrs. Lancaster does. I just don't want to see anyone taken advantage of while they are helping."

Could she trust him? Should she trust him? Did she have a choice? She'd started off on this impossible search because she'd been desperate enough to cling to a rumor and hope, but she hadn't the slightest idea what to actually do now that she was here. "I'm afraid all I have is a letter mailed from here several months ago."

"Doesn't sound like that close of a friend," Mr. Banfield muttered.

"Doesn't sound like a very helpful sentiment," Margaretta returned.

"Mrs. Fortes—"

"Mr. Banfield, as Mrs. Lancaster so helpfully noted, I am weary from my travels. Perhaps your dissection and belittlement of my life could wait until tomorrow? You can stare at me suspiciously while I dust the shelves and assure yourself I've no intention of absconding with candlesticks."

His eyes widened, and then he coughed, possibly to cover a laugh, but she frankly didn't care anymore. Up these stairs was a chair that wasn't moving that she could sit in while she ate and a bed she could snuggle into afterward. At the moment, those two things sounded like bliss.

And if she imagined what it would have been like if the handsome Mr. Banfield had been as welcoming as the elderly grocer, well, that was no one's business but her own.

Three

Nash sat in his office, trying to return to the work he'd been doing before Mrs. Fortescue had blown into town. He stared out the big window beside his desk, looking across High Street to the now quiet inn where the stage had unloaded hours earlier.

The ink on the tip of his quill had dried, so he gave up pretending and dropped the feather onto the desk surface.

A trio of children ran down the street chasing a dog and inspiring a small, sad pang in Nash's chest. Had his sister's baby lived, he would be about the age of those boys. But he hadn't lived and neither had Mary. And for a few years after, it had been a question of whether or not the husband she'd left behind would survive the loss. Nash had been prepared for his good friend to slip away like his father had after the death of Nash's mother, alive only in the most literal sense of the word.

It was a cruel twist that the baby his mother had died bringing into the world was felled by the same fate.

The boys shouted as the dog turned abruptly and began chasing them, yapping happily as they scattered down a side street.

Nash smiled at the antics even as he silently reaffirmed his commitment to remain free from the sort of entanglements that killed men while they were yet breathing. This town was his family. It gave him purpose and companionship. When the Lord called him home, there would be people who mourned. That was enough.

He was still watching the quiet street when Mrs. Lancaster shuffled past. He nodded to her when she caught his eye, and she smiled back. Eventually the walk back to the cottage she'd lived in with her husband would become too much for her and she'd have to move into the rooms above the shop, but for now she seemed content to travel back and forth up the hill each day, even though she had to come into town at an exceptionally early hour because Nash never saw her in the morning until she was sweeping the stones in front of her door.

Her walk home tonight, however, meant Mrs. Fortescue was now alone. Her unfettered access to whatever possessions Mrs. Lancaster had in the upstairs rooms was a nominal concern at best, but he still fought the urge to take a walk in that direction. Whether it was to make sure the downstairs doors were locked or that the woman on the run was safe by herself, he wasn't sure, and that question was enough to drive him away from the door and back to his desk.

The tin of peppermints in his jacket pocket rattled as he settled into his chair. He shifted to the side and fished them out, frowning at the tin before dropping it into a drawer. Metal clinked as it landed on top of the tin of peppermints he'd bought earlier in the week.

He was going to have to come up with a better reason to go by Mrs. Lancaster's shop tomorrow. If he bought any more peppermints, Mrs. Lancaster might hurt herself from laughing so hard. She'd barely contained her mirth this afternoon, and it had given him a modicum of pleasure to inspire the old woman to smile, even though that wasn't a very difficult task.

Mrs. Fortescue's near laugh flitted through his mind. How much more heroic would it feel to be the one to make *her* smile and laugh?

Nash shook his head. Why did it feel comfortable to be a bright spot in Mrs. Lancaster's day but decided uncomfortable to consider being such for Mrs. Fortescue? His commitment to himself was certainly strong enough to withstand being the source of a full smile on a young, pretty woman.

Wasn't it?

Noises from the street below were the first thing to break into Margaretta's sleep-soaked brain the next morning, but she kept her eyes pressed closed until she could work through the lingering fogginess. She was in a bed, that much she knew, but where the bed was located was still trapped in the black shrouds of drowsiness that were threatening to creep back over her consciousness.

The bedding was clean and smelled of fresh air and lavender, an unfamiliar but certainly not unpleasant combination.

She turned her attention to the vague noises that had woken her in the first place. Definitely not London. Raised voices, horses, and wagon wheels were all distinct from each other, instead of a large noisy blur. A small town then, or a less busy side street of a larger one.

A frown pulled her eyebrows together and sent cracks running through the last vestiges of sleep. Why wasn't she in London? She remembered traveling to Margate, but the sounds reaching her ears weren't those of the seaside resort town, either.

With great care she eased one eye open to look at the plain white walls and heavy, dark wood timbered ceiling. The visual inspection of her surroundings brought everything she'd done in the last three days swirling back. Complete consciousness caused something else to swirl as well, though, and she clamped her eyes shut again while taking deep, slow breaths and willing the seizing of her midsection to cease.

Once she had her body somewhat under control, she opened her eyes again to take in the room she'd done nothing but glance at the evening before. She hadn't known where the candles were and the energy to search for them had seeped from her very bones. After eating most of the bread and half of the fruit she'd purchased downstairs, she'd undressed and climbed into bed.

And apparently slept through the night and into the morning.

Not too far into the morning, though, based on the paleness of the light creeping through the uncovered window.

A low groan rumbled up from Margaretta's chest as she stretched and pushed herself to a sitting position on the side of the bed.

"Good morning."

Margaretta screamed and fell back onto the mattress, flinging the bedding up as if it would create a shield. After two heaving, terrified breaths, she eased the blanket off her face and looked toward the door. She had to peek over her feet as well as the blankets since her legs were now sticking over the edge of the bed at an odd angle.

Her heart pounded in her ears, drowning out whatever greeting Mrs. Lancaster was giving her as she brought in a small tray bearing a plate of toast and stewed apples, as well as a sturdy mug with steam curling over the rim.

With a hard swallow and a deep breath to calm her racing heart, Margaretta sent up a quick prayer that the steaming mug was a proper cup of tea. How she longed for a good cup of tea. The inns between mail stages had served something they called tea, but could more accurately be described as dirty water. Yet another thing she'd been taking for granted in her former life.

She pressed a hand to her middle. How quickly things could change. Hopefully, one day she could return to such a life, though it would never be the same for her after this experience.

Margaretta pulled her legs in and pushed herself up to sit against the plain wooden headboard. "Good morning." She cleared her throat to ease the croak in her voice. "What are you doing here?"

Mrs. Lancaster chuckled while she arranged the tray and eased herself down to sit on the edge of the bed. "Why, I live here, dear. I've got a cottage up the hill, but my old bones don't like making that walk early in the morning, so I come back here to sleep every night. I was afraid I'd disturb you when I retired last night, but you didn't so much as shift a finger."

Margaretta lifted the mug and inhaled the steam, further quieting her senses. She cast her eyes about the room, taking in the carved wardrobe on the far wall and another small bed situated on the other side of the window from Margaretta's. Staying in rooms run by the older woman was one thing, but actually living with her? Did Margaretta want to do such a thing? How long would she be able to keep her secret if she was living in such close quarters with Mrs. Lancaster?

She only had another month or two with her secret anyway, but by then she hoped to have a better plan than wait and see if it was a girl. If only it didn't take so long to have a baby. The solution to her predicament would be much easier if she could simply hide away for a month or two and have the whole thing over with before anyone realized she wasn't in Margate after all.

Of course, having the baby was only the beginning of her problems. The question was what she was going to do with it afterward, particularly if it turned out to be a boy.

There was no way that Samuel would accept another person sliding in between him and his father's title.

As she nibbled on an apple, hoping her breakfast would stay settled, she looked around the room once more. "I didn't take your bed, did I?"

Mrs. Lancaster waved a hand in dismissal. "One bed's as good as another. I never know which one I'll decide to crawl into until I come up here each night anyway. At least with you here, I'll have a bit of predictability in my day."

While Margaretta ate, Mrs. Lancaster talked, sharing funny stories from the many years she'd been living in the town, tossing in a mention or two of a specific townsperson's connection to more influential people, thankfully none whom Margaretta had ever met. There were tales from various markets, though if all of them were completely true, Margaretta would eat the plate her toast had been brought on.

Behind a screen in the corner, Margaretta washed the travel dirt off as best she could and dressed, taking care to shift her clothing so no one could see the slight swell in her midsection. After wearing the same dress for three days straight, it was bliss to feel clean clothes against her skin.

With Mrs. Lancaster unable to see her face, Margaretta tried to bring the conversation around to the women Mrs. Lancaster had supposedly helped over the years.

"There hasn't been that many, in truth. We take care of our own here in Marlborough, and it isn't often that women travel through by themselves."

A rustling cloth indicated that Mrs. Lancaster was setting the bedroom to rights. "Mrs. Wingraves' girl comes through and cleans up here every day, but she won't bother your things."

The only identifying or valuable thing Margaretta had was the valise, and she wasn't overly worried about a young country girl seeing it. The chances of her recognizing the stamped metal emblem or the custom craftsmanship were limited. She wanted to talk more about Mrs. Lancaster's girls, though. "Do you remember meeting Katherine?"

"I don't often exchange first names." Mrs. Lancaster chuckled. "Shall we place wagers on what Mr. Banfield plans to come in and buy today?"

Margaretta came out from behind the screen to find Mrs. Lancaster smiling at her. The old woman winked before retreating into the other room.

Obviously Katherine and the other girls were not open for discussion this morning. In a way, Margaretta was glad. She wouldn't want Mrs. Lancaster freely telling people about Margaretta's presence, either. The older woman apparently had no problem talking about the solicitor, though, and Margaretta needed to know if he was going to be a problem. "Does he stop by every day?"

"Hardly ever." A cackle shook the other woman's shoulders. "But he'll be in every day as long as you're living here."

Margaretta couldn't help but wonder what it would be like to have someone willing to go to that much trouble to watch over her. "He must care about you a lot."

"Probably more than he'll admit. Makes my heart break to see the man try and harden his heart. Bible's full of people with hard hearts, and I wouldn't want to be a single one of them."

Margaretta didn't know what to think of the way the old woman sprinkled God and the Bible into her conversation as casually as a Londoner might mention the traffic or haze. Even though she'd been attending church her entire life, Margaretta hadn't ever thought to make Jesus quite that versatile. She'd left Him in church where He seemed to belong, but Mrs. Lancaster appeared to think He belonged everywhere.

Margaretta listened to more stories as the women went down the stairs and into the back of the store.

"There's a broom and dusting things in this cabinet. The broom at the front is just for the porch. I sweep it off regularly. Helps cut down on the amount of sweeping we have to do in here and lets me know what everyone's doing in the town."

Mrs. Lancaster laughed to herself as she moved to the front of the store. Margaretta had never met someone who seemed to be so continually . . . happy. Despite everything going on in her life, all the uncertainty around her future, Margaretta couldn't help but smile. With her steps feeling a bit lighter, she opened the cabinet and tried to guess what was used to clean which things.

The wavy glass that covered the front of Mrs. Lancaster's shop kept Nash from seeing any particular details, but it was clear that at least six women milled around near the front of the store, waiting for Mrs. Lancaster to help them. It was also clear that none of them were Mrs. Fortescue. Not that he'd had that much time to observe her, but none of them moved like her or even stood the way he remembered her standing.

Besides, she was supposed to be cleaning. Not shopping.

He slipped quietly through the door and eased it shut behind him so as not to draw notice of the chatting customers.

Was it possible Mrs. Fortescue had decided to leave already? Mrs. Lancaster's voice was as cheery and helpful as ever, so if the young woman had departed it must have been in an amiable sort of way. Otherwise, the old shopkeeper would have been spouting proverbs to everyone along with their purchase totals.

No, if she were still here, she'd likely camped herself in the back with the knick-knacks and other non-food goods. Someone on the run wouldn't want to be near the front when this many people were in the store. Nash nodded a greeting to one of the women and strolled around a set of shelves to head toward the back portion of the store.

Mrs. Fortescue was in the deepest corner, trying to juggle a brass barometer while running a cloth over the space it had occupied.

Afraid that his sudden presence would cause her to drop it, Nash crept up and lifted it from her arms. She was still startled, but at least the barometer didn't break as a result.

The rest of the shelving nearly did, though, when she squealed and spun around to press herself against the boards, her hand pressed to her chest and her breath coming in quick, short bursts. "Mr. Banfield," she gasped. "You gave me a fright."

"Obviously." Nash nodded at the now clean shelf behind her and held up the barometer. "May I?"

"Oh!" She scurried away from the shelf. "Of course."

"Why aren't you using the goose feathers?"

Mrs. Fortescue blinked at the cloth in her hand, coated with dust she'd just raked from the back corner of the shelf. As they both stared at her hand, a large fluffy grey clump drifted off the rag to the floor. She sighed. "Now I'll have to sweep again."

Nash's eyebrows rose. "You already swept? Before you dusted?"

Pink stained her cheeks. "No, of course not." She pushed her shoulders back and straightened her posture but then immediately slumped and folded forward again before turning back to the shelf. After shaking the loose dust from her cloth, she started on the next section. "What do you need, Mr. Banfield? I'm afraid I can't help you procure any goods. You'll have to wait in line with everyone else."

"And if what I came for was information?"

She snuck a glance at him. "I'm afraid I can't help you with that, either."

He settled his shoulder against the wall and fought a grin. This was almost fun. Where had the suspicion and worry from yesterday gone?

Was the considerable but misguided effort she was putting into cleaning the shelves enough to convince him she meant the shopkeeper no harm? It must have been, because all he felt when he looked at her was a swelling drive of curiosity. He really wanted to know who she was looking for, what she was running from, and why Marlborough had been the point between the two. It was enough to convince him that keeping her close was a very good idea.

"What if I didn't ask anything about why you were here?"

Mrs. Fortescue laughed, but it was brassy and bitter. She stopped pushing dust around to cross her arms over her chest. "What else could you possibly have to ask me?"

What did he have? His interest in learning about her felt vague and undefined. "Obviously cleaning is not something you're especially good at."

She looked like she wanted to smile but managed to restrain herself. "And I imagine you are perfection personified at everything you attempt?"

"Hardly." He smiled. He couldn't help it. She was so appealing when she smirked or smiled or anything really that chased away that desperate air she'd had about her when she got off the stage. Had it really been only yesterday? He leaned in as if he were imparting a secret. "I am absolutely terrible at shooting."

She went back to dusting, but her attention clearly wasn't in it. "That must make hunting parties nervous."

He shrugged and moved his way down the wall, staying close to her as she cleaned. The tasseled saddlebag on the shelf in front of him was crooked, so he reached out to straighten it. "I am, however, rather exceptional at riding, so they let me come along and chase the hounds. And now it's your turn to throw humility aside and confess what skills you're hiding."

What was he doing? Was he actually flirting with her? He hadn't even considered participating in a flirtation in years. And now he was doing so with a woman he barely knew, one he wanted to run out of town? It didn't make any sense, but he realized he was, possibly for the first time in a very long time, having fun.

"I cook."

Of all the things he'd have guessed she would say, cooking was the last one he expected. "You cook?"

She nodded.

"Well, perhaps I can get you to bring me nuncheon one day."

She blushed but said nothing. He didn't really expect her to. The idea had been planted in both their minds, spoken without any real thought behind the words, but now the idea of a pretty young woman stopping by the office to brighten his day and share a light meal with him was too enticing by far.

He needed to get out of here and think about what he was really doing.

"I'll be back tomorrow, Mrs. Fortescue. And here's fair warning that I intend to weasel out of you your favorite type of pie." He settled his hat on his head and tipped the brim. Then he turned and strode out of the store before she could say anything.

Four

Margaretta ran the goose-feather duster around the jars of spices with a practiced swish. She wasn't an expert at cleaning by any means, but in the past week and a half she'd learned a thing or two about effectively dusting the shelves.

She'd also learned how stubborn charming old women could be. No matter what she asked, Mrs. Lancaster wasn't telling her a thing about whether or not she'd met Katherine. Margaretta wasn't getting very far on her own, either. The current postmaster for the town had taken up his post only six months ago. Even if he had the memory of an elephant, he wasn't going to remember a girl posting a letter before he took the job. She also couldn't risk strolling through too many public areas because while Margaretta was looking for Katherine, someone else was looking for her.

More swishes of the duster accompanied her self-pitying sigh and sideways glance toward the front of the store.

He was late.

No matter how good she got at dusting, it was never going to be a chore she particularly loved. It seemed to pass much faster when Mr. Banfield stopped by to chat though, which he'd gotten into the habit of doing every day, just as the morning rush of customers subsided. It was why she'd altered her cleaning routine to save the back shelves for his arrival.

But today he hadn't come, and the sun had already passed its peak in the sky.

"Margaretta, dear," Mrs. Lancaster called from the front of the empty store. "I've something I need your help with."

Margaretta stored the duster back in the cabinet before going to the front of the store. Whatever the old woman needed, Margaretta was happy to do, or at least attempt to do. She'd been an utter blessing from the Lord.

A short laugh escaped through Margaretta's smiling lips as she shook her head. She was even beginning to sound like the old woman, thanking the Lord for things in the middle of the week. The truth was, though, that Margaretta didn't know what she'd do without the woman and everything she'd done for Margaretta. If that wasn't the definition of a blessing, she didn't know what was.

"Ah, there you are. I've got a delivery for you to make." Mrs. Lancaster set a small basket, filled to the top and covered with white muslin, on top of the counter.

Margaretta took the handle with a bit of trepidation but found that while it was heavy, it was manageable. "I'm afraid I don't know my way around town. I haven't ventured much past the store and the church yet."

The church had been another one of those places Margaretta had been hoping to catch a glimpse of Katherine. She'd spent more time inspecting the rows of people than listening to the rector the past two Sundays. No familiar blonde runaways had been in attendance.

Mrs. Lancaster waved a hand in the air. "It's not far. Just a bit down High Street."

"I'll need better directions than that." Margaretta smiled. She took a deep breath and plunged on, hoping she could catch Mrs. Lancaster off guard and get a bit more information to help in her search. She was convinced the old lady knew something or she would have simply told Margaretta that she didn't know Katherine FitzGilbert. "Perhaps you need me to go by wherever Katherine stayed when she came through town?"

A pudgy, wrinkled hand waved through the air. "We've plenty of time to discuss this search of yours later. Right now we've got a quiet moment, so it's the best time to make a delivery. Just turn right and head down High Street. You can't miss Mr. Banfield's office. It's got a big window looking out over the street."

"Mr. Banfield?" Margaretta choked. What could possibly need delivering to him? He'd been in the store every day for the past ten days. Except of course for Sundays and then they'd seen him at church.

"That's correct. He was supposed to come in and get it this morning, but something must be keeping him. I don't mind going out of my way for one of my best customers."

Or sending Margaretta out of her way, as the case may be. "I know what you're doing."

Mrs. Lancaster's grin was infectious. "Good. Then you won't mess it up. Off with you now."

Margaretta laughed as she put on her pelisse and tucked the basket against her hip before setting off on her journey. Who needed subtlety when they had Mrs. Lancaster's charm?

His office was easy to find, and Margaretta enjoyed the short walk through town. She'd seen the market twice now from the window above Mrs. Lancaster's shop and both times had been an assault on all of her senses. The quietness of the rest of the week appealed to her more. It was an odd blend of feeling like the city and the country at the same time.

She took one last deep breath of fresh air before pushing her way into Mr. Banfield's office.

He was bent over his desk, the quill flying across the paper in tight, neat writing. She waited until he'd paused to clear her throat to catch his attention.

The bewildered expression on his face was darling. He looked from her to the window to the clock on his mantle. "Oh! I'm late." A blush rode his cheekbones. "Well, not late because I didn't have an appointment, but—"

"Mrs. Lancaster sent you this." Margaretta offered him the basket.

He took it apprehensively but broke into a wide smile after he pulled back the muslin. "Hungry?"

"What?" Margaretta's eyebrows pulled together until she looked into the basket to find a variety of fresh foodstuffs, including a loaf of the apple bread she'd made last night and a fruit tart left over from this morning. "I could eat."

That was almost a joke. She could always eat these days.

Still, it was nice to sit at the small table Nash led her to and dig into the basket with a handsome companion.

Not that she thought him handsome. Oh, very well, she thought him handsome. Who wouldn't with that shock of dark hair that didn't seem to want to lay right and blue eyes framing a strong, straight nose? Of course she found him handsome, but she didn't think it meant anything.

"And what has you working so diligently this morning, Mr. Banfield?"

He held up a section of apple bread. "Did you make this? It's amazing." He shoved another morsel into his mouth. "If you're going to be delivering me freshly made tarts and bread, you might as well call me Nash."

She looked around the office to keep from having to look directly at him. A blush was already threatening, and it would take over her complexion if her gaze remained locked with his. Bookshelves lined one entire wall while stacks of newspapers and magazines covered every other available surface. Obviously he kept abreast of news far beyond the borders of Marlborough. "I've never been in a solicitor's office."

"I would think not. It's not the normal domain of gently reared females."

He was fishing for information again, but she let it pass. She couldn't really blame him. The curiosity hadn't seemed rooted in any malice since her first day in town. That didn't mean she answered, though. Even if she found herself wanting to.

"It's an interesting look into your life."

Nash looked around with her. "What do you mean? It's mostly books and papers."

She turned back to him, wondering if her smile looked playful. Part of her felt like an imp, but the other part of her was really and truly curious to know what went on behind those serious blue eyes and shaggy dark hair. "You've a partner desk but no partner. That seems a rather poignant bit of symbolism."

He snorted a laugh and dabbed at his mouth with a napkin. "I assure you that it's not. It's simple practicality. The partner desk has more drawers."

The words were spoken lightly, but he still shifted in his seat, rolling his shoulders as if his jacket was suddenly uncomfortable. Had she hit the nail a little too close to the head? Was he alone in this world by something other than choice? A feeling of dread licked through her stomach before she could stop herself from wondering. Did he have a woman in his life who had left him heartbroken?

Not that Margaretta was in any sort of condition to mend it, if that was the case, but still. She hated to think of Nash hurting.

"You won't answer if I ask about your friend."

It was a statement, not a question but Margaretta nodded anyway. Katherine had disappeared in the midst of devastating rumor and scandal, the kind that ruined a girl's future. The letter Margaretta had gotten was essentially a good-bye. An assurance that Katherine had left of her own volition and was safe but wouldn't be returning.

Margaretta hoped that meant Katherine had figured out how to have her baby and protect both of them while she was at it. She'd also managed to stay hidden for eight months. Margaretta needed to know how she'd done both of these things.

Nash broke off another piece of apple loaf. "What about your husband?"

Margaretta's eyes opened wide. "What do you want to know?"

It was quiet for a few moments, Nash not meeting her eye. "Did you love him?"

They were getting too close. She was only in this town for a little while, and for the time she was here, she was essentially in hiding. Any sort of relationship with this man, even friendship, was unwise.

She murmured something about getting back to Mrs. Lancaster and rose from the table, leaving him to do whatever he wished with the remaining food.

Still, she stopped at the door and looked back at him.

He was watching her with softness around his eyes. Accepting what she was willing to give him without pushing for more. How had they come so far so quickly? Was a half hour of conversation here and there enough to make two people closer in such a short time?

It was. She knew it was because it had happened. Was happening. And since she wasn't willing to give him anything else, she gifted him the one thing she could. "Nash," she swallowed and licked her lips, "you can call me Margaretta. And no, I didn't love him."

And then she left.

Not knowing what else to do, Margaretta took the next two weeks to try to venture into the more public areas of Marlborough. She scurried along the edges of the market, looking at every vendor and shopper, heart pounding that she'd find someone she knew, but it wouldn't be the right someone. The trepidation she expected to feel at her continued lack of success never came. It was easy to forget, in her cozy rooms and quaint little village, that a real sense of urgency was needed.

The fact that Mr. Banfield didn't miss a single visit over those two weeks didn't hurt. Nash. Margaretta kept waiting for him to push more at the door she'd opened and ask about her husband, her family, but he never did. Instead their discussions had grown more playful and personal, the illusion of privacy the back shelves gave them lending itself to long stretches of uninterrupted conversation.

They swapped childhood stories, though Margaretta was careful to never mention the leather shop or horses. They talked about the Sunday service. They even got into a rather heated, good-natured debate on whether or not the new style of longer, looser trousers for men would become acceptable formal evening wear.

And he watched her. She knew he did because she couldn't stop herself from watching him, too. For a woman who had been comfortably settled with the idea of having her father arrange a marriage for her, the giddiness that ran through her when she heard Nash greeting Mrs. Lancaster was both foreign and exciting.

But as time crept on and her stay in Mrs. Lancaster's rooms extended into its second month, she felt uneasy. They'd been good weeks, if strange, and her days had fallen into a routine.

They would wake early and eat breakfast before going down to the shop. Mrs. Lancaster never seemed to mind that Margaretta came down after her, choosing to wait and dress after the older woman had left the rooms. The mornings no longer left her middle feeling queasy, but it was requiring more artful arranging and fastening of her gowns to keep everything hidden.

Then she spent the day cleaning and avoiding the customers until Nash came to visit. Afterward, she would straighten the shelves and come upstairs to prepare dinner.

When Mrs. Lancaster closed the shop, she would come up and eat and then go for a long walk by herself. Margaretta offered to accompany her a few times, but Mrs. Lancaster always turned her down, saying a lone walk was good for digestion and reflection.

Margaretta spent the evenings reading or trying out a new bread or tart recipe. She'd taken to making baskets for Nash to pick up when he came into the store.

Then she would fall into the bed and not wake until the sun hit her eyes the next morning.

At least, that had been the pattern until three days ago.

Sleep had become an elusive friend, almost as difficult to find as Katherine was, and her body was feeling the loss.

Margaretta lay in the bed, listening to the deep breathing from the bed beside her. The fits and lulls of momentary unconsciousness she managed to find at night couldn't have accumulated to more than a couple of hours if they'd been strung together. The level of exhaustion she'd been feeling every day should have meant she slept blissfully each night, but the stillness of the night and the way the town actually quieted with the setting sun only gave her time to think about all of the things she pushed aside with the busyness of the day.

More than a month in Marlborough and she was no closer to finding Katherine than she'd been on day one. But she hadn't a clue what to do next. Mrs. Lancaster would talk about anything and everything under the sun except for Katherine. Whenever

Margaretta raised the topic, it was brushed aside like the dust and dirt she'd gotten so good at cleaning.

Who else could she ask, though? Aside from Nash, she knew no one in town, and had deliberately avoided more than passing greetings with them all. Asking Nash would mean having to answer all of the questions they'd been dancing around. As close as they'd gotten, she couldn't ask for his help without expecting to give him some answers in return.

So where did that leave her? She was running out of time.

Margaretta pushed the covers down below her hips and pulled her nightgown tight across her middle. The false sense of security and comfort that hiding away with Mrs. Lancaster provided was shrinking, and Margaretta's middle was starting to swell. It wasn't much yet, certainly not anything a little slump and dress adjustment couldn't hide, but it was difficult if not impossible to ignore anymore. How much longer before she would have to find a way to procure new dresses? How many more days could she linger before she had to find a more permanent place to hide? If Samuel found her, there'd be no denying her condition soon.

Worries swirled in her head until she felt dizzy. She knew what Mrs. Lancaster would say, because she'd been listening to the woman prattle on for weeks. The shopkeeper would say that worries belonged to the Lord since He stayed up all night anyway.

The thought brought a smile to Margaretta's lips. A nice concept, letting someone else stay up and worry for you while you slept blissfully all night through.

She glanced over at the other bed, and the woman whose shape she could barely make out in the moonlit room. Mrs. Lancaster always left the drapes open, stating that the sun was ever so much nicer to wake up to than having Mrs. Berta Wheelhouse come round and tap on her window with that long stick of hers.

People like Mrs. Wheelhouse probably existed in London, going around and waking people at the appointed times in return for a small fee. Margaretta had never had to concern herself with that, sleeping as late as she wished for most of her life. If there was a need to rise at a certain hour, one of the servants saw to waking her. She'd never thought to wonder how they woke on time.

Right now, though, the room was dark, even with the open curtain, so the moon must have set, and the sun would soon start pinkening the sky. Then she would have to find a way to haul herself from this bed once more and go about cleaning the shop downstairs. Again. The chore was considerably more difficult than she'd expected it to be. Especially when she was fighting the desire to simply curl up in a ball in the corner and let the rest of the world carry on without her while she took a nap.

As exhausted sleep finally smothered the constantly swirling concerns, Margaretta had one last fleeting wish that she could return to those lazy mornings and let this sleep last for hours.

Five

Bright sunshine made Margaretta wince the next time she tried to open her eyes. She sat up quickly in surprise, and instantly regretted it as the sudden movement sent her running for the chamber pot for the first time in more than a week. Once she could move comfortably again, she looked around the room.

A shard of sunlight cut across the wall and onto Margaretta's pillow from the bright beams edging around the dark green drape that had been pulled across the room's little window.

Rapid blinks were required to keep the sudden moisture in her eyes from turning into a bout of weeping. She'd been struggling with that a lot lately, had even had to claim to get dust in her eyes one or two times when the urge to cry had hit her while in the shop below. But this act of caring on Mrs. Lancaster's part when Margaretta was feeling so alone and bereft was simply too much, and a few drops of emotion leaked from Margaretta's eyes before she could contain herself.

A small smile tilted her lips, forming a track for the salty tears, and she wiped them away idly with her wrist while she pulled the curtain to the side and looked down at the town she was coming to know.

Mrs. Cotter was walking down the street with her mouth set in the determined line she always got when she was planning on haggling Mr. Abbott about paying less for bread. She always visited the baker just after midday in the hopes that he'd be worried about selling everything that day. It never worked, but she kept trying.

Margaretta blinked. Could it possibly be noon already? Had she slept that long? If so, she'd missed her talk with Nash for the first time. What had he thought? What excuse had Mrs. Lancaster given him? The idea that Nash might think her the type of slothful person who would laze a day away just because she felt like it made Margaretta sad. He knew her better than that by now, didn't he?

A loud shout drew her attention to the right and the large three-peaked inn she took care to avoid. Its location in the middle of High Street meant that people from London were frequently coming and going from the center of town on their way to or from the popular city of Bath.

The stage pulling up in front of the inn now was nicer than the one Margaretta had traveled on, though still loaded down with as many people as it could carry. It wasn't a mail coach, so there was more room for people and luggage, and passengers scrambled down from every nook on the roof and sides. Finally, a footman stepped up to open the door to allow the interior passengers to disembark.

A man with thick, graying hair stepped out before settling his tall hat back upon his head. Even from this distance, she could see his hawklike nose and the sun glinting off the silver embroidery of his waistcoat.

Her gasp seemed to pull all the air from the room while squeezing all of the breath from her chest. She'd thought she had more time—that her story would hold for at least another few weeks—but there was no denying that her father was in Marlborough. She hadn't wanted to worry him, hadn't wanted him to blame himself for the fact that the man he'd married her to had a crazy brother who would do anything to move up from third to first in line for the title of Viscount of Stildon.

If Samuel Albany found out she was expecting his older brother's child, he'd either beat it out of her or find a way for it to meet an early demise once it was born. He'd all but told her as much when he paid his condolences after the death of his brother, John.

If there hadn't been so many witnesses to John's accident on the gangplank of the *HMS Malabar*, Margaretta would wonder whether Samuel had had a hand in it as well. But no, that had simply been an unfortunate incident, though the move from third heir to potential spare seemed only to whet Samuel's appetite for the title.

If her father was here, did that mean he knew she was no longer in Margate? Did Samuel know she was no longer in Margate? That she'd stayed there for a mere three days before the sight of Samuel's manservant sent her scurrying across the country on a circuitous route of mail coaches?

The *ifs* piled up until she began to feel sick again, but then the bottom fell out of her stomach entirely as another man emerged from the coach. A shorter man with a rounded hat already on his head. He stepped to the side and pulled spectacles off his face before taking a handkerchief from his pocket and cleaning the road dust from the lenses.

Margaretta tried to swallow, but her throat was dry.

Samuel was here. And her father was with him.

Nash was working, trying his best not to worry about Margaretta, whom Mrs. Lancaster had said was feeling poorly this morning. Was she very sick? Did she need a doctor? Would she even be willing to see one? Until now, she'd been very particular about where she would go outside of Mrs. Lancaster's shop. If she wasn't trying to find her friend, Nash doubted she'd have gone anywhere other than church and that only because Mrs. Lancaster all but dragged her there.

The opening of his door was a welcome distraction, especially since he didn't know the two gentlemen who walked in. Strangers would consume his whole attention and force him to stop thinking about a particular dark-eyed, dark-haired fugitive.

Nash cleared his throat and set his quill aside on a stack of last week's newspapers before rising to his feet. "May I help you, gentlemen?"

The two men looked around Nash's admittedly messy office. Nearly half of his clients communicated with him via messengers, and most of the others were locals who were just as likely to have him over for tea as to meet in his office. Over time, he'd allowed the room to become a bit cluttered, though he still considered it quite professional. Would it look as such to two obviously well-to-do men from London?

Whether they decided it was professional or not, it must have passed muster because the younger man gave a stiff nod, and the two men came to stand by Nash's desk.

The older of the two men cleared his throat and glanced sideways at his companion. Tension ran underneath that gaze, and Nash couldn't help but remember the last tense, secretive person who'd walked into his life unexpectedly.

So much for the visitors distracting him from thoughts of Margaretta.

"As a man of the law, I assume you are man of discretion?"

Nash's eyebrows flew upward. How long had it been since someone questioned his character like that? When everyone knew everyone in a town, your reputation tended to precede you. "Of course," Nash stated. Was there really any other acceptable answer? "Have a seat, gentlemen."

They all made themselves comfortable in Nash's chairs, though the younger man's eyes never seemed to settle on anything for more than a moment.

The older man nodded and swallowed before clearing his throat again. "We need you to facilitate a meeting with the local providers of transportation. We need to inquire about moving about the country with a bit of, er, discretion."

A more vague and ridiculous request Nash had never heard. There was definitely something else going on here. He'd simply have to go along with their ridiculous wording until he learned what it was. "Of course. My name is Mr. Banfield."

The younger man sneered. "We assumed as much, Mr. Banfield. Your name is on the sign after all."

"Yes," Nash said slowly. "But as you did not come equipped with the same type of signage, I assumed we wanted to introduce ourselves like gentlemen."

"Yes, yes, of course," the older man said quickly. "This is Mr. Samuel Albany, third son—"

"Second son!" snarled the younger man.

The older man's eyes hardened and his shoulders stiffened. "Third son," he repeated with deliberate enunciation, "of the Viscount of Stildon. His elder brother, John, is recently deceased, however."

Mr. Albany's snarl deepened as he locked eyes with the older man. Their gazes didn't hold for long, though, and soon Mr. Albany was back to staring at the bookcases.

The old man gave a small nod and turned his attention back to Nash. "I am Mr. Curtis Fortescue of Fortescue Saddlery."

Thoughts pinged around Nash's brain like bullets shot into a metal bucket. He'd heard of Fortescue Saddlery, of course; everyone had. They were known for crafting beautiful, sturdy saddles as well as high-quality bridles and harnesses. Their leatherwork was exceptional... which brought to mind Margaretta's unique valise. He'd only gotten a glimpse of it that first day, but her last name and her overprotectiveness of the leather satchel merged with the presence of the men in his office. Nash had a feeling he was one step closer to finding what she was running from.

And how hard she was running.

The saddles were exclusively used by England's richest, noblest families. Anyone connected to that business wouldn't have the need to work in a shop. But how was she connected? Was this man her father-in-law? Or, Nash swallowed to ease the rising burn in his throat, was she possibly not widowed after all?

Mr. Albany swiveled his head in Nash's direction. "Fortescue Saddlery has partnered with my family to extend their line of saddles. We intend to take the racing world by storm and wish to travel anonymously until we choose to reveal the connection."

"Thus the discretionary transportation," Nash clarified. Now he knew for sure that these two were playing some sort of game. Marlborough was the last place anyone with a connection to horse racing would care to go. For that matter, Wiltshire as a county probably wasn't high on anyone's list. There was only one track of note in the whole county, and it was a good bit south of Marlborough.

If one was looking for a person, however, someone who would be looking to go somewhere with as many traveling options as possible, one couldn't do much better than Nash's little town.

"Yes." Mr. Fortescue turned toward Nash, but his gaze flickered almost constantly in Mr. Albany's direction. "We're exploring ways to travel around the southern half of England without anyone knowing we're there."

"And you wish to talk to the people who might help you do that?" Nash asked.

The two men looked at each other, both frowning, both seeming to be trying to glare the other into some sort of submission. Mr. Albany was the one to finally break the glare and answer. "Yes."

Nash couldn't tell which man actually held the power in the pairing, and that made his job considerably more difficult. Of course, it would be much easier if he knew what his job was supposed to be in this instance, because he was fast coming to believe that his role in this little tableau was to protect Margaretta. There was no doubt in his mind that she was who these men were really looking for, but Nash couldn't tell what they wanted to do when they found her.

Tension spiked up his neck until he was forced to roll his head along his shoulders to relieve it. He tried to cover the movement by reaching for a piece of paper and a quill, though he had no idea what he was going to write.

"I can certainly arrange for you to meet with a few people who might be amenable to arranging your travel needs." It wouldn't be difficult to keep them away from anyone who knew anything about Margaretta. Her dealings with the townspeople had been limited mostly to the women who came into Mrs. Lancaster's shop.

"All of them," Mr. Fortescue bit out. "We wish to speak to all of them."

Nash's eyes widened. "We've more than a dozen inns with stage stops in Marlborough alone. When you include the neighboring towns and villages, that number goes up considerably. Then there's the smiths and stables that rent out horses and carriages and—"

"This is ridiculous." Mr. Albany surged from his chair and paced to one of Nash's overflowing bookcases. "Your discretion is costing us precious time, Fortescue."

Mr. Fortescue's eyes narrowed. "And what alternative would you suggest?"

Nash waited, not daring to even breathe, but both men lapsed back into an angry silence, glaring at each other. Finally, Nash cleared his throat to break the tension. "If you'll give me your names and where you're staying, I should be able to make some arrangements within the next day or two." He looked from Mr. Albany back to Mr. Fortescue. He was an older man, but he carried himself well. He could be Margaretta's father or husband, possibly even her father-in-law, and Nash desperately needed to know which. "Are you traveling with wives, gentlemen? I would be happy to suggest a few entertainments for them while you are in the area."

"Women are a nuisance," Mr. Albany muttered while Mr. Fortescue looked at Nash with assessing brown eyes that went a long way toward convincing Nash he was looking at the father and not the husband. The shape and color were too familiar to Nash for this man to be anything other than a blood relation. Why give her name as Fortescue, then? The idea that she might not have married at all crossed Nash's mind, but he dismissed it. He had no reason to believe she'd lied to him at any other time than possibly that first day. And then it would have been understandable.

"The only woman in my life," Mr. Fortescue said slowly, "has been taking the waters for the past two months to see to her health."

Mr. Albany emitted a sound of disbelief. "Should have sent her to my estate in Shropshire. She'd have been safer there."

"Have you reason to believe her health is in danger where she currently is?" Mr. Fortescue asked pointedly.

The men were staring at each other again, struggling for power. What would happen when one of them actually came out on top? If Margaretta was caught in the middle of these two gentlemen, he could see why she would run away.

"I'm sure I wouldn't know," Mr. Albany finally said quietly. "But then again, neither do you."

Another tense moment passed before Mr. Albany straightened his coat and strode toward the door. "We're staying at The Castle Inn. My man arranged rooms for us there."

Mr. Fortescue's skin faded to a sickly gray that matched his hair. "Your man is in town?"

"Is that a problem?" Mr. Albany's eyebrows lifted, along with the corners of his lips. The smile was smug and even sent a shiver down Nash's back. "I've been sending him ahead of us to scope out the prospects. He seems to think this town very promising."

"Tonight." Mr. Fortescue snapped at Nash. "I want the first meetings arranged by tonight. We'll spend no longer in this town than we absolutely have to. You may join us for dinner with the details of the arrangements."

"Quite right," Nash said slowly, though he wasn't really sure what he was agreeing to. All he knew was a moment ago he'd been sure that these two men were the threat Margaretta was running from, but now he'd just learned there was a third man. One who might have been in town for a while.

It was a grim prospect indeed.

It was nearing evening before Nash managed to enter Mrs. Lancaster's store. By then he was nearly trembling with worry. He'd wanted to go straight there after the men had left his office, assure himself that Margaretta was tucked away safely in the rooms upstairs, but knowing there was a third man, an unknown who Nash couldn't recognize, made him cautious. On the chance that he was being followed, Nash visited stables and talked to the innkeepers who dealt with the stages and mail coaches.

Every time he'd considered running for the store, he'd see a stranger or lock eyes with one of the townspeople he didn't know as well and cautiousness won out over panic and made him put every effort into looking as normal as possible. But now sufficient time had passed, and he couldn't stand the wait anymore. He had to see her.

She'd had a month—more than a month—to decide he was trustworthy and tell him her problems. Now that he'd been thrown into the middle of them without a single clue, she was going to give him answers.

Assuming, of course, that she was still safely tucked away above the shop.

Frustration and worry ate at him until his composure and patience crumbled, leaving him vulnerable and angry. He was nearly shaking with the emotions as he strode down High Street with the wind whipping his coat about. Rain was probably blowing in. It seemed to be that sort of day.

The store was blessedly empty when he walked into it. In fact, the only person he could see was Mrs. Lancaster.

"Where is she?" He knew the blatant question would give the meddling woman ideas, but he'd handle that later. She was already assuming whatever she wished. Right now, he needed answers, and he desperately needed to know that Margaretta was safe.

"Upstairs." Mrs. Lancaster shuffled toward the door and turned the sign to *Closed*.

"Are you certain? Have you actually seen her today?" Nash forced himself to breathe more slowly. What if they only thought she was upstairs and she'd actually been found by Mr. Albany's man or run away again so that they wouldn't catch her?

Nash couldn't wait for Mrs. Lancaster to work her way around whatever clever phrasing she felt like giving him today. He had to see Margaretta, had to know the worst thing that had happened was that she'd caught a head cold. He tore through the store and out the back door. He was two treads from the top of the stairs before he realized what he was doing. Was he really planning on storming up here, invading what was essentially her home? A gentleman didn't do such a thing.

The sick feeling he'd had when Mr. Fortescue's skin had paled welled up within Nash's gut once more until it squeezed his heart. Gentleman or not, he had to see Margaretta.

His pause had given Mrs. Lancaster time to catch up with him, though, breathing a little harder than Nash would have preferred. "Can't have you up here without a chaperone," she huffed before reaching past Nash and pushing the door open. "We've a guest, dear!"

A groan came from deep within the rooms, sending panic through Nash. Had Mr. Albany's man already been here? He nearly pushed Mrs. Lancaster into the front room, which acted as a sort of parlor and kitchen area. A worktable was positioned along the wall near the fireplace, and cooking hooks sat empty along one edge of the hearth. An iron rack cut across the middle of the fireplace opening. Three chairs sat around a dining table, while three more created a little seating area near the window. A door across from the fireplace stood open, and that was where Margaretta appeared, looking so pale that her thick dark brows and red lips stood out in shocking contrast.

"Nash, er, Mr. Banfield?" Her dark gaze swung from Nash to Mrs. Lancaster and back again. "What's going on?"

Relief took the strength from Nash's legs, and he braced an arm against the wall, forcing breath into his lungs. She was well. Everything was going to be fine. On the heels of relief came determination. Whatever was going on, he could keep her safe, as long as she finally gave him all the answers. But how to convince her to do such a thing? He'd asked more than once about her life, her past, and she'd proven to be quite silent on the subject, so trying to be delicate it about it was something he didn't have the time or inclination to do. So he decided to throw the largest rock he could into the pond and see what ripples it created. "I think it's time you told us about your husband."

Six

Margaretta's insides clenched once more as a dozen possibilities tumbled over themselves in her mind.

Why was Nash pushing for information now? He'd been so patient. It couldn't be a coincidence that his urgency came on the same day Samuel and her father came to town. One or both of them must have encountered Nash.

But how? Why?

She couldn't believe her father would go alone with any scheme of Samuel's. He'd said he believed her when she told him she was afraid of Samuel. It was why they'd agreed to send her to Margrave in the first place.

But now with both of them here together, she didn't know what to think.

"My husband is dead." She choked out the words around the knot of fear that had settled in her throat the moment she'd seen Samuel exit the carriage.

Nash drove his fingers through his hair before folding his arms over his chest, emphasizing the breadth and strength of his body. It was something Margaretta had quietly admired, his ability and willingness to do more for his clients than sit behind a desk and draw up paperwork. He walked all over town and involved himself in the more physical aspects of property management. But what did he intend to do with her?

"And your connection with Fortescue Saddlery?"

A chill wrapped around Margaretta's body despite the fact that she could hear Mrs. Lancaster poking at the fire, building it up until it crackled once more. What could she say? Nash had become a friend—she wouldn't let herself consider him anything more than that—and it wasn't as easy to lie to him as it had been when she first arrived in town. But keeping her father's business interests intact was the main reason she'd disappeared instead of asking him to help her. If he ended the business deal with the Albany family racing stables, it could ruin his reputation and his business.

Margaretta licked her lips. "I . . ."

He stared, face hard but devoid of any readable expression. Margaretta swallowed, wondering if, once he learned the truth, his sense of honor would compel him to tell her father she was here. What would her father do? He'd seemed confident that everything would work itself out when she'd last seen him, but now he was here with Samuel Albany of all people. What did that mean?

"Please don't lie to me," Nash whispered hoarsely, his blank expression giving way to a glimpse of the agony she heard in his words. "Because I'm fairly certain there's a bag in that room behind you that proves it."

She stared back at him, locking her gaze with his, trying to decide what she could say while desperately hoping he could hear all the things she couldn't bring herself to put into words.

The hiss and pop of boiling water followed by the rattle of crockery startled Margaretta, allowing her to finally look somewhere other than Nash's blue eyes, swirling with indeterminate emotion. She turned to see Mrs. Lancaster making yet another pot of tea. It was the only thing Margaretta had been able to keep down today, and Mrs. Lancaster had been running upstairs every hour and a half or so to make a fresh pot.

"Margaretta." Nash's quiet voice had lost the note of pleading, replaced by gentle strength.

She slumped against the doorframe, feeling tired and weak despite the amount of time she'd spent in bed today. An equal amount of time had been spent at the window—watching, waiting, hoping that her father and Samuel were simply passing through and would be taking the stage out of town.

They hadn't.

"Yes," she whispered, closing her eyes and letting her head fall against the wall. "I am connected to Fortescue Saddlery."

"And the Mr. Fortescue I met today? The one I'm supposed to be meeting for dinner in an hour?"

Margaretta swallowed, knowing her lies were about to catch her completely. "My father."

His eyes widened. "Why give us your unmarried name?"

Mrs. Lancaster bustled in and wrapped an arm around Margaretta's shoulders. "What does it matter right now, can't you see the poor girl's dead on her feet?"

Once Margaretta was in the vicinity of one of the chairs, she collapsed into it, unwilling to look at either of the room's occupants. Right now, these were her only two friends in the world, and she couldn't bear it if she saw distaste or distrust on their faces.

A cup of tea was pressed into her hands, and she sipped it gratefully, letting the hot liquid soothe her tight throat and settle her jumpy stomach. After half a cup, she almost felt normal again.

Perhaps the tension of waiting to be discovered had been making her more ill than the baby or some other illness.

"It's no wonder she's unwell," Mrs. Lancaster crooned, smoothing a hand over Margaretta's hair. "She hasn't slept nigh a wink in at least three days."

"How would you know?" Nash asked.

That pulled Margaretta's attention from her teacup. Didn't he know she'd been living here with Mrs. Lancaster?

The old woman chuckled. "It's hard to miss when my bed's barely five feet from hers."

Nash's head jerked toward the door to the small bedroom. In two steps he was standing in the doorway, hands braced against the frame and leaning in to look over all the contents of the room. What did he see? Margaretta and Mrs. Lancaster were fairly neat—Margaretta more so because she didn't have enough possessions to make much of a mess, but the room was lived in.

His expression was incredulous as he looked over his shoulder, still braced in the doorway. "You're living here."

"Of course I am." Mrs. Lancaster set about cleaning up the tea, but kept her gaze averted from both Margaretta and Nash. The lack of eye contact was unusual and unnerving.

"But I see you walking toward your cottage every evening. You even wave at me through the window." Nash's tone was cold enough to pull Margaretta's attention once again. How in the world had this confrontation become about Mrs. Lancaster instead of her? "Why aren't you living in your cottage?"

It wasn't hard to guess why he was angry. Mrs. Lancaster's lonely evening walks had probably included a very deliberate path by Nash's office. As a man who liked to control everything, he certainly wouldn't like being fooled by an elderly shopkeeper. Despite the tension, Margaretta had to hide a small smile behind her teacup. Mrs. Lancaster was certainly sly.

The sly woman currently under Nash's scrutiny set down the kettle and turned to face him, her hands planted on her soft hips, making the flowers on her muslin print dress bunch together. "Because I leased it."

Silence fell, so stark that Margaretta didn't even risk taking a sip of tea. Even the fire refused to pop or crackle.

Nash's mouth pressed into a tight line. "You leased out the cottage?"

"Just said as much, didn't I?" Mrs. Lancaster bustled over to the worktable, her right foot dragging a bit with each step but looking as spry as someone half her age otherwise. She pulled a loaf of bread toward her and began slicing it. "I leased it to a lovely young widow and her companion." She gave a nod in Margaretta's direction. "Friends of yours, if I had to guess."

So Mrs. Lancaster had known something about Katherine! Hope surged through Margaretta only to fade as the full implications of Mrs. Lancaster's statement sank into Margaretta's weary brain. "I'm afraid you're mistaken. My friend isn't a widow."

"Nonsense." Mrs. Lancaster slid the slices of bread onto the rack over the low-burning fire. "There's more than one kind of widow, you know."

Margaretta glanced at Nash to see his eyebrows climbing up toward his hairline. "There is?"

"Of course. There's the woman who got married and then found herself without a husband." Mrs. Lancaster jerked her head in Margaretta's direction. "Then there's the one who simply doesn't want anyone to ask too many questions."

"So your tenant lies?" Nash frowned.

Margaretta bit her lip. Knowing how passionate Nash was about his clients' property agreements and contracts, the thought of Mrs. Lancaster, whom he felt so personally responsible for, making such an arrangement without him, and to someone potentially unscrupulous, had to be torture.

Mrs. Lancaster shrugged. "If you're narrow-minded in your definition of widow."

Margaretta blinked. How could the definition of widow be misconstrued?

Nash grunted in disdain, obviously agreeing with Margaretta's reaction. "She is a woman whose husband is dead. I'm fairly certain Johnson's *Dictionary of the English Language* will support me in that statement."

"And why does he get to decide?" The old woman's wrinkled hands settled onto her hips again and a frown pulled down the corners of her lips, making her round, normally cherubic face look distorted. "Besides, how do you know she's not a widow? There's no age limit on them. A woman can get widowed in a month if her husband ups and dies on her."

"Or less," Margaretta muttered. She didn't know if either of them could hear her, but the fact that she'd been married less than two weeks—a mere eleven days—had to be something of a unique achievement. And given that seven of those eleven days had been spent apart while he prepared to leave the country, she'd barely been married at all.

Nash glanced at her, and for a moment Margaretta thought he would latch onto her statement and demand more answers. Instead he sighed, rubbed a hand across his face, and looked back at Mrs. Lancaster. He must have decided her news was the most pressing. After all, Margaretta was someone he could dispense of with a simple visit to the inn where her father was staying.

She swallowed. Would he do that? Did he want to be rid of her? Would he even care to hear the rest of her side of the story? The intense desire to go back and change the last five weeks coursed through Margaretta. If she could, she would trust Nash sooner, break her silence and tell him everything. But she couldn't go back, and her time may have run out while she waited.

"Mrs. Lancaster, you just told me your tenant was lying."

Margaretta looked from Nash's frustrated expression to Mrs. Lancaster's determined one. This argument was going to be fruitless, but at least it was proving a good distraction for everyone in the room.

"Well, what do I know? I'm an old woman." Mrs. Lancaster scurried to the fireplace and picked up an iron rod from the hearth to poke at the dying flames.

Nash cleared his throat and ran a hand along the back of his neck. "Which is why we agreed to let me handle your legal documents. I never saw this lease."

"Of course you didn't." She used a long fork to flip the bread on the rack. "Because I didn't have one written up."

Margaretta laughed before she could stop it, and even though she quickly muffled it with both hands, it was enough to draw Nash's attention back to her once more.

An answering smile started to curve his lips, and the skin at the corner of his eyes crinkled before he shook his head and looked at the ground. A deep breath expanded his chest until she could see it pulling against the seams of his jacket. When he looked up again, his demeanor was serious once more but no longer appeared angry. "You can't do that, Mrs. Lancaster."

"Why not? It's my cottage."

Nash sighed. "Are they even paying you?"

Mrs. Lancaster shrugged. "We have an agreement. They uphold their end and I uphold mine." She glanced at Margaretta. "Well, usually I do. I just told Mrs. Fortescue here about her friend's presence, but she's been here long enough that I trust she means no ill will toward her friend."

"Of course not," Margaretta whispered. All this time Mrs. Lancaster had been helping her, she'd been trying to decide if Margaretta was worthy? If it was safe to take her to Katherine? Her hand drifted down to her midsection, an urge that grew daily that she tried her best to ignore. Did Mrs. Lancaster know Margaretta's secret?

Her eyes cut to Nash. Did he know? Mrs. Lancaster had just revealed that Katherine hadn't wanted anyone to know she was here, yet Mrs. Lancaster had told not just one but two people. "What about Nash?"

"Oh, him?" Mrs. Lancaster sent him a wink and waved her hand as if disregarding his presence. "He can't help himself from protecting the innocent and disadvantaged. Keeping your friend a secret has almost been more about protecting him than her. Last thing he needs is another project." Her eyes cut to Margaretta. "Unless it's the right one."

Nash frowned. "I'm going to the cottage."

Before Margaretta could blink, Nash was striding toward the door, his boots hitting the floor with dull thuds.

"Wait!" Margaretta didn't know where the sudden burst of energy came from, but she surged out of the chair, laying a hand on Nash's shoulder. "What about your dinner with my father?"

Yes, the cottage and Katherine and everything she'd just learned was important, but Margaretta also needed to get her father and Samuel out of town. And the sooner Samuel did whatever he came here to do, the better.

Nash's eyes cut briefly to where Mrs. Lancaster was collecting the barely warmed bread from the rack and throwing a handful of dirt on the fire. It didn't take long for him to look back at Margaretta, though. "I'll tell him urgent business came up with another client. No one was available to talk to him and his partner until tomorrow morning anyway, so he'll simply have to accept the list then."

"Partner?" Margaretta choked out. Her father could not have accepted Samuel as a partner.

Nash's brows drew together and the worry that had covered his face when he'd first entered the rooms returned. "Companion? I don't know. There was something going on that I couldn't understand. And I don't know what any of this"—he gestured between himself and Mrs. Lancaster—"has to do with any of that"—his hand swung toward the window overlooking High Street. "But I know I can get at least a few answers at the cottage tonight."

Mrs. Lancaster pressed the two pieces of bread into Margaretta's hands on her way to the door. "Well, you're not going anywhere without me. It's my cottage after all."

"And you are my responsibility," Nash answered. "I promised your husband."

She flipped one hand through the air. "The dear man's dead. What he doesn't know can't hurt him."

Nash opened his mouth to answer but closed it with a sigh.

Margaretta bit off a piece of the toast, the first thing she'd actually felt like eating all day. As her two friends headed out the open door, a tingling crept up from Margaretta's feet. Could the woman in the cottage actually be Katherine? Could Margaretta risk waiting to find out? Her father and Samuel would be ensconced in their inn by now, preparing for dinner. Was there really much risk in her leaving the shop?

Clasping the unfinished bread in one hand and grabbing her cloak off the wall hook with the other, Margaretta ran out the open door just before Nash could close it behind them. She took a deep breath and looked from a frowning Nash to a smiling Mrs. Lancaster.

"I'm going as well."

Nash and Mrs. Lancaster looked at her, their expressions as different as could be. The concern in Nash's face warmed Margaretta's heart, settling her stomach even more. "I don't know." He sighed. "Mr. Albany said his manservant was in town. I didn't—I don't like this situation and I'd rather you stay here until I know more about it."

Mrs. Lancaster pushed past Nash on the little landing. "Of course you're coming, dear." She draped the large yellow cloak over Margaretta's shoulders and flipped the hood up to cover the dark curls. "It's your friend we're looking for after all."

And if Katherine could disappear once, she could disappear again. Eight months ago, she'd left society so completely that Lord FitzGilbert didn't even acknowledge her existence anymore. What was stopping her from running again if she learned Margaretta was in town?

"No," Nash said. "It isn't safe." He reached for the older woman's shoulders, the care in his gesture easing the lines of frustration and anger on his face. "First, we're going to see what business you've mucked up with your cottage."

"I've mucked up nothing." Mrs. Lancaster sniffed. "Everything is exactly as I wish it to be."

Nash closed his eyes and sighed again.

Mrs. Lancaster took the opportunity to head down the stairs. Margaretta followed before Nash could lead her back into the safety of the little rooms she'd been clinging to all day. It would be better if she stayed behind, there would certainly be less risk, but seeing Mrs. Lancaster standing up to Nash, revealing all she'd managed to do without anyone knowing, had given Margaretta a bit of courage.

Yes, life had thrown her a problem, but it was time she took steps toward solving it. Even if the person in Mrs. Lancaster's cottage wasn't Katherine, Margaretta was done waiting for someone else to tell her what to do. She'd been hiding behind Mrs. Lancaster's care and even Nash's protectiveness, hoping to find an old friend who would give her an easy solution. It was time she found one of her own.

By the time they reached the alley at the bottom of the stairs, Mrs. Lancaster was nearly skipping like a child on a treasured outing while Nash practically stomped his way down the uneven stone pavement.

Margaretta considered the future as she trotted along behind the others, occasionally stuffing a bite of bread into her mouth. Part of her was still exhausted from the emotional and physical toil of the day, but hope was a powerful animal and she would ride it as long as it allowed her to run after her companions.

It wouldn't be so bad, being a country matriarch. True, she'd never lived anywhere in her life besides London, but it wouldn't be such a bad life if she could establish herself in a little village, grow old, and then force everyone to her will the way Mrs. Lancaster seemed to be doing. It was the last thing Samuel would expect her to do. There had to be some way she could establish herself somewhere, perhaps a village less passed through by aristocrats and London's wealthy elite.

The idea of leaving Marlborough, leaving Nash, made her heart pound in her chest again. Or perhaps that was the fact that they were getting farther away from the safety of the store. Yes, that had to be it, because with the baby, she couldn't afford to form any attachments that might influence her thinking.

They strolled down narrow alleys and back lanes, Mrs. Lancaster waving a greeting to everyone she saw. Several people seemed to be on their way home for the night, probably planning their dinners and when to put the children to bed.

Lack of physical energy forced Margaretta to slow her steps a bit, and she fell back. Every few steps, Nash would glance back and adjust his pace so she wasn't too far behind him, but Mrs. Lancaster simply shuffled on, her skirts doing an odd swish with every drag of her right foot.

As they moved out of town, the businesses and shopfronts gave way to rows of homes. The buildings became simpler and the road a bit rougher, especially on the hill away from the market area. Tile still graced the walls that weren't made of brick, but the mouldings became plain and the structures more square. Some even seemed to tilt from the weight of age.

Could Katherine really be living in such a place? While Margaretta had flitted on the edge of society, Katherine had been exceedingly popular before her fall from grace. Could she have left behind the jewels and dozens of servants to live in such reduced circumstances?

Immediately Margaretta knew the answer was a resounding yes. If the rumors were true, if there was even the slightest accuracy in what they said, then there was every possibility that Katherine had turned her back on all she knew. Given the chance, Margaretta certainly would. If it meant the difference between death and survival for the innocent life she carried, she'd sweep and dust until she couldn't hold a broom. The simple life hadn't been as bad as she'd feared.

And if anyone had enough resilience to make it work, Katherine did. It was why Margaretta was here. She had to know how Katherine had managed to make it all work.

Had to know if there was a way to redeem such an impossible situation.

The road they were climbing suddenly opened up, spilling them into a large open green area lit brightly by the sun perched on the horizon. Homes surrounded the green, and a few children chased each other with long, flat paddles, their game of cricket abandoned in the name of pursuit.

"William," Mrs. Lancaster called, "does your father know you've run off with his cricket bat again?"

One little boy stumbled to a halt, dirty blond hair flopping into his eyes. He bit his lip, revealing a gap where one of his front teeth had fallen out. "No, Mrs. Lancaster."

"Well, then." The old woman braced her hands on her knees. "You rush home and do an extra good job brushing your father's horse tonight and we'll say nothing about it."

The little boy grinned, revealing a second hole in the lower half of his smile, and rushed across the green to hug Mrs. Lancaster.

Margaretta felt a pang in her chest at the sight of the happy little boy. Whatever had pushed her to find the strength to walk up that hill drained away. She hadn't thought past the fact that she was going to have a baby, hadn't let herself imagine what came next because she simply didn't know how to protect such a dependent, helpless being.

She hadn't let herself consider the fact that the baby she was carrying would one day, God willing, grow up. Be a child. Run around and play cricket.

Unless Samuel Albany found him first.

Seven

Nash took a deep breath. He knew the children running around on the green, getting hugs from Mrs. Lancaster before running off to their homes. Of course he knew them. They even shouted their greetings in his direction as they ran off.

He always found it a bit difficult, though, dealing with the children. Awkward. The younger they were, the more he wondered whether or not their mothers had suffered in bringing them into the world. It was always a vague uncomfortableness, a hazy impression of guilt that inspired him to keep a modicum of distance between himself and the younger generation.

Tonight, however, his unease didn't feel so very abstract. It felt specific. Personal. And he wasn't sure why.

His sister's boy would have been older than the ones currently running away from the green, but that didn't stop him from wondering what his life would have been like if she had lived, if he'd watched her son run around the green with a cricket bat. If she and Lewis had grown their family. What would that have meant for Nash?

He'd likely have married. But watching Lewis nearly let go of life had convinced Nash that perhaps the danger was a bit too great. Perhaps it was a risk not worth taking. Without a child to hold, a future to cling to, Lewis had given himself over to the melancholy for almost three years.

His business had faltered and he became nearly destitute. Friends and family had been worried, trying to deal with their own mourning while at the same time encouraging Lewis to keep living.

Eventually, he had started living again. Turned his business around, remarried, even had two young children.

Despite his recovery, one thing Lewis said during those three years had stayed with Nash beyond any of the other painful ramblings. Lewis hated himself because he'd been the one to do that to Mary. His loving Mary had eventually killed her.

Nash didn't think he could live with such a sentiment.

Especially now that the vague emotion was starting to sharpen into a familiar face. Was that what had him thinking so much about Mary and Lewis tonight? Margaretta's presence at his side? The one woman who had cracked his resolve ever so slightly?

As the children ran off, laughing and happy, Nash thought through the families they represented. Many of them had brothers and sisters who hadn't lived through infancy. Two had lost their mothers—one to childbirth and another to illness.

Despite this, the families seemed, for the most part, happy and healthy. But sometimes pain could fester unseen, allowing you to fool the world at large.

The last boy disappeared over the rise, leaving Nash alone with his obscure remnants of pain.

Margaretta squeezed his arm and offered him a small smile, a soft look in her eyes that seemed to reassure Nash that he wasn't alone. She didn't even know why he hurt, what he'd vowed, but she could sense his inner torment. The fact that he wanted to wallow in that sympathy, to lean into her and seek the comfort of her presence, shocked him out of his stupor.

Mrs. Lancaster. The cottage. The mysterious tenants who didn't seem to actually be paying their way for anything. These were the things he needed to be focusing on.

The cottage wasn't very far from the green, just two turns down a rutted side street, and they were standing before it. The walls tilted slightly, showing the age of the house. When it had been built originally, it had probably stood alone, overseeing a sheep pasture outside the village, but Marlborough had grown to eventually swallow the pasture and the house.

Margaretta's breathing increased even though their pace remained slow. The harsh rattle of her shallow breaths concerned him, as did the fact that she'd grown so pale that her face was nearly translucent.

He fell back a step to stand near her but resisted the urge to take her hand or wrap an arm about her for support. Despite the depth of their conversations over the last weeks, he'd never touched her. Never sought to bridge the distance between them. If he did that, if he changed the tenuous definition of their association, he was afraid he'd forget the vow he made to himself and his sister, the quiet promise he'd made to the town that became his family.

Mrs. Lancaster lifted one fisted hand and rapped her gnarled knuckles against the thin wooden door.

The panel swung open to reveal a pretty girl about Margaretta's age, with blond hair pulled into a simple bun and a pale green muslin dress that had once been fine but was now showing wear from multiple washings.

Nash fell back half a step as Mrs. Lancaster pushed into the doorway, cooing over the baby in the woman's arms. The woman said nothing, simply stared at Margaretta, eyes wide and expression blank.

The baby gurgled as Mrs. Lancaster continued her attentions.

A hard lump settled in Nash's throat. Babies made him even more nervous than young children did. Babies meant that very recently a woman had potentially been at death's door and only God's mercy had kept her from it, though how God decided which mothers got to live was beyond Nash's understanding.

Margaretta reached over and clasped her fingers around his hand. The feel of her skin against his, even if it was only their hands, nearly broke the wall he'd constructed around his heart. Her nails dug into his palm, but the sharp pain didn't disguise the warmth of her touch or the softness of her hands. She'd run out tonight without her gloves, and every detail of her skin implanted itself on his brain without waiting for his permission. His thumb traced over a spot that was beginning to roughen and callus because of her daily use of a broom.

Margaretta had every ounce of his attention, but he didn't have hers. She was staring at the woman in the doorway, her mouth moving but no sound coming out. Finally she managed to swallow and clear her throat. "Katherine."

"Margaretta." The blonde, apparently the missing Katherine, licked her lips before pressing them into a firm line. Her voice was flat, and when she finally pulled her gaze from her Margaretta, she spared Nash only a glance before glaring at Mrs. Lancaster.

The angry stare didn't bother the old shopkeeper, who was too busy with the baby to pay much attention to the woman holding him. "As lovely as the weather is, dear," Mrs. Lancaster said, finally straightening away from the baby, "perhaps you could invite us in? The chill of night is coming, and we don't want darling Benedict to catch cold."

Katherine's gaze cut to Nash once more before she looked over her shoulder into the depths of the cottage. Tension pulled her face tighter, making the lines of her neck stand out. But then she nodded and stepped back into the house, leaving the door open in silent invitation.

Nash considered leaving. If he hurried, he'd only be a few minutes late to his dinner meeting. But before him, if he were willing to brave a room containing a baby, were the answers to all Margaretta's secrets. This was who she'd been looking for. Her quest was complete. She could soon be leaving Marlborough, and Nash didn't want to be asking himself *what if* for the rest of his life.

With a sharp inhale that did nothing to steady his heartbeat, he followed Margaretta over the threshold.

Margaretta didn't realize she'd grabbed Nash's hand until she had to let go in order to follow Mrs. Lancaster into the cottage. She had to make a conscious effort to let go of him, but she wasn't going to miss her chance to talk to Katherine, and Nash didn't seem in any hurry to follow their hostess into her home.

The interior was considerably darker than the street outside, and Margaretta blinked to accustom her eyes to the dimness and to the unexpected surroundings. She remembered visiting Katherine in London, remembered the silk-hung drawing room, the plush Aubusson carpet in her bedchamber. The contrast between those memories and the stark simplicity in front of her now was startling.

The wide-planked wood floor was swept clean, and two plain but comfortable-looking wooden chairs flanked a fireplace, where a fire burned low. On the other side of the room, a smooth wooden table, a bench, and three more chairs sat in front of a basic kitchen work area. Two doors led from the room, presumably to the bedchambers.

Even assuming that the chambers in the back of the house combined to the size of the room in the front, the entire living space was smaller than the double drawing room in Katherine's father's house where Margaretta had attended more than one social gathering.

Mrs. Lancaster moved comfortably about the room, taking the baby in her arms and making her way to a rocking chair in the far corner. It was obvious she had done more than give these women a home. She'd been visiting them with some frequency, probably when she'd taken those long evening walks.

Margaretta stared at Katherine. Her old friend stared back. From the corner of her eye, Margaretta saw Nash shifting his head back and forth as he looked from one woman to the other. How strange it must seem to him that she'd been so desperate to find this woman and now that she had, she was saying nothing.

What could she say, though? How did one broach such a subject?

"I see the rumors are true." Margaretta winced. That had probably not been the best way to open the subject.

Katherine's eyebrows lifted, and she looked over her shoulder to where Mrs. Lancaster was rocking and cooing at Benedict. One side of Katherine's mouth tipped up into a sad smile. "Not as true as you think."

The baby let out a gurgle that slid into a bit of a whimper, as if to call Katherine's statement a lie. Margaretta said nothing, allowing the circumstances to ask her questions for her.

"Mrs. Lancaster didn't tell me you were here." There was an undeniable note of censure in Katherine's voice, even if the look she sent Mrs. Lancaster's way was edged with indulgence.

"Of course I didn't, dear." Mrs. Lancaster never looked up from the baby. "You'd have taken this precious boy and made a run for it. When I said I'd protect you, I never said that didn't include protecting you from yourself."

A sigh that could almost past for the beginning of a laugh deflated Katherine's chest as she looked at the floor and shook her head. When she finally looked up, her expression was a little softer. "Won't you sit? You may select a chair from the table if you wish to join us, Mr. Banfield."

The man choked. "I beg your pardon; have we been introduced?"

The impish smile that flitted across Katherine's face was familiar enough to send a pang of sadness through Margaretta. Would her own smiles soon become a mere memory? Something that only hinted at the carefree girl she used to be?

Hadn't they already become so? Her smile had returned easily after her husband's death. Perhaps a bit too easily. But then they'd hardly known each other, had both considered the marriage a prudent match that would secure a future between Fortescue

Saddlery and Albany's racing stable. John's death, though tragic, had seemed more of an inconvenience than a devastation, but then it became apparent that Margaretta's future hadn't simply been delayed. It had been threatened.

She hadn't smiled much since.

Katherine sat in the other chair flanking the fireplace, looking as serene and graceful as she had during her Season in Town. "I make it a point to know all the important people in my area, Mr. Banfield," she said smoothly. "Besides, Mrs. Lancaster speaks highly of you." She then turned toward Margaretta. "How have you been?"

"Well." Margaretta said hesitantly. "I've been married."

Katherine looked like she didn't quite know what to do with that information. "Congratulations."

"And widowed," Margaretta continued.

"Oh." Katherine's eyes widened, and her hands gripped each other in her lap. "I'm so sorry."

As the baby let out another loud cry, the door behind Katherine opened, and another young woman stepped out. Margaretta's jaw went slack. She recognized the woman with the round face and the nondescript brown hair as the friend who had followed Katherine around almost like a companion. "Miss Blakemoor?"

The woman blinked in Margaretta's direction. She coughed. "Miss Fortescue?"

Nash, who had stood upon the other woman's entrance, shot an accusing look Margaretta's way. A reminder that he hadn't forgotten the news that had been dropped on him earlier this evening.

Margaretta cleared her throat. "It's Mrs. actually."

Miss Blakemoor coughed and darted a look in Mr. Banfield's direction. "Oh, er, I'm actually a Mrs. as well."

The dizzying weakness from earlier crept into the edges of Margaretta's brain as she tried to make sense of everything she was seeing and learning. What was real? What was pretense? Perhaps if she gave a little information the woman, or apparently women, she'd come to see would provide some answers as well. "Mine was a very short marriage," Margaretta said with a smile that attempted to break the tension in the room. "It is sometimes difficult to remember I received a new name."

Nash crossed his arms over his chest and narrowed his eyes at her. "What else are you forgetting?"

"Nothing that need concern you."

"Too late. I find my concern growing by the moment."

Margaretta stared at her hands. He sounded almost hurt, as if he, too, had found himself in a strange place these last few weeks, wondering about their burgeoning friendship. Had he grown feelings for her the way she was deathly afraid she'd grown feelings for him? Margaretta wasn't willing to name the thing that made her heart pound whenever she heard him greet Mrs. Lancaster during his daily visit. To do so would mean one more thing she had to leave behind when the time came.

The baby cried once more, this time refusing to be hushed and calmed by Mrs. Lancaster. "I do believe he's hungry, my dears, and I'm long past the age of being able to help him with that."

Margaretta clamped her teeth together to hold in her shocked laughter, while Katherine and Miss Blakemoor felt no such compulsion to restrain theirs. Nash emitted a low groan.

Miss Blakemoor crossed to the rocking chair and lifted the bundle in her arms. "I'll see to him, Mrs. Lancaster."

And then she disappeared back into the room she'd come from.

Katherine looked at Margaretta pointedly. "Rumors rarely get everything correct."

Nash pulled his chair over to the grouping and settled into it. "Are you from London as well, Miss FitzGilbert?"

Katherine's pointed look narrowed into a glare as she shifted her gaze to Nash. "How do you know my name? Yours is blazoned across the sign outside your office. Mine, however, is certainly not."

"Margare—er, Mrs. Fortescue, I mean—" he cut himself off with a sigh and pinched the top of his nose as he took a deep breath. "Margaretta came to town looking for a Miss Katherine FitzGilbert. As she appears to have been looking for you, I'm assuming that you are the Miss FitzGilbert in question. Or have you suddenly remembered a name change as well?"

Katherine pressed her lips together. "No name change, but I would thank you to forget you ever heard mine."

He lifted one eyebrow. "I never forget anything."

The look he shot Margaretta's way made her sweat.

Mrs. Lancaster popped up from the rocking chair. Nash rose slowly as well, his eyes staying on Margaretta the entire time. She'd come to learn his different expressions in the past month, but this one was unreadable. What was he thinking?

"As long as we're all making confessions here this evening," Mrs. Lancaster said, stepping closer to the chairs where Katherine and Margaretta sat, "we might as well get one more out of the way. Then we can all start to move on from this secrecy."

Margaretta didn't know how she felt about the word *confessions*. Uncovering of secrets was probably more accurate, since none of the parties involved had given their information voluntarily, but if Mrs. Lancaster had something she felt she needed to say, Margaretta certainly wasn't going to stop her. The woman had been a blessing, and she deserved peace if some secret was tormenting her.

"Of course," Margaretta said. "You can tell us anything. I believe everyone here can say they owe you loyalty."

Nash and Katherine both nodded, their faces mirroring the concern and confusion Margaretta felt.

"That's nice of you, dear, but it's not my confession." She smiled as if whatever she said next would be the best news in the world. "It's yours."

Margaretta's mouth dropped open as she looked in Mrs. Lancaster's kind, smiling eyes. The woman looked almost excited about putting Margaretta on the spot. Or was it the news she expected to hear that made her so happy? Margaretta's attempt to swallow almost choked her. The shopkeeper knew. How long had she known? How long had she suspected?

"I . . . I . . ." Margaretta looked over at Nash but quickly dropped her gaze to the floor. "I'm sure I don't know what you mean."

"It's why you're here, isn't it?" Margaretta could hear the frown in Mrs. Lancaster's voice, and it made her wince. But then one wrinkled hand landed on her shoulder and gave an encouraging squeeze.

Why couldn't she say the words? Margaretta swallowed. It wasn't as if she'd done anything wrong. She had been married. But somehow she knew the news would change everything. Yes, she'd never claimed to be anything other than a widow, but other than that one conversation, she and Nash had never acknowledged her past. Once he knew the truth, there'd be no ignoring it. "I . . . I can't."

Another squeeze encouraged Margaretta to look up into the face of the woman who had filled the role of friend and mother for the past five weeks. "It's time," Mrs. Lancaster said. "You might as well tell everyone about the baby."

Eight

"Baby?" Nash shot to his feet. He looked to the door where the woman whose identity he hadn't known had disappeared with the baby. Surely they weren't trying to say that the baby was Margaretta's, were they?

When he finally pulled his gaze back to Margaretta and saw her hand pressed to her middle in a gesture he remembered his sister doing countless times, the bottom fell out of his world.

Images and memories he'd kept locked away flooded to the surface. The joy and laughter that abounded when Mary and Lewis had shared their news. More laughter, as well as the occasional good-natured complaining, as she'd grown too large for public outings and never seemed to be able to find a position that stayed comfortable for more than five minutes.

The devastation when Lewis came to Nash's house and simply sat, unable to bring himself to say the words and actually tell Nash what had happened.

Miss FitzGilbert finally coughed, breaking the silence before speaking into it with a quiet voice. "You were actually married, weren't you?"

Margaretta didn't stop looking at Nash. He wished she would. Then maybe he could stop looking at her as well.

"Yes." Her voice was just as low and quiet as her friend's. "I married Mr. John Albany, and we spent three days at his father's country house in Surrey. Then we returned to London so he could prepare to leave with his regiment. They were to set sail from London one week after we came home."

She swallowed visibly. "He slipped on the gangplank and hit his head. By the time they could fish him out of the Thames, he was dead."

No one said anything. As the shock of Margaretta's announcement wore off, questions filled his mind, warring with a mixture of other emotions.

"A tragedy to be sure," Katherine said quietly, but without the sort of emotion one would normally expect behind such words. "But why are you here? You've nothing to hide."

Margaretta closed her eyes. Tears welled along the compressed lashes before streaming in twin tracks down her cheeks. "John's younger brother wants nothing more than his father's title." Her eyes opened, deep brown pools of utter despair. "If he finds out I'm with child, he'll stop at nothing to make sure the baby never has a chance to inherit."

Nash grabbed on to the back of the chair, gripping it until his knuckles whitened and the wood threatened to break the skin. The uneasy feeling he'd gotten in his office that morning grew to a spine-tingling premonition. The man who had come to his office, traveling with her father, inquiring of discreet modes of transportation. If that was him, if that was the brother . . .

The implications slammed into Nash faster than he could process them. If what Margaretta said was true, what in the world was she going to do?

Margaretta pressed her hand against her middle, where the softness she'd known her whole life had given way to a firmness that wouldn't let her forget the impossible situation she was in. It was the crowning example of the fact that life was not fair. She'd done everything right, all that was asked of her, and still this had happened.

Somehow, once she started telling the story, finally admitting it all, it felt less daunting. The last vestiges of the hope that had carried her to Katherine helped stem the tears that were dripping onto her skirt. She also couldn't stop the story now that she'd started, even if she wanted to keep as much as possible to herself and only answer the questions they asked. In a fit of nerves and energy that propelled her from the chair and sent her pacing across the floor, the words poured out of her.

"Of course, his family was anxious to know if it was possible a baby had come from the brief union. John's older brother left for India years ago and married there. He and his wife have been to England to visit a time or two, but there's been no children. John knew he was likely to inherit, but he joined the navy anyway. Our marriage was more of a business union than anything: Fortescue Saddlery and the Albany racing stables. It made sense."

She took a deep breath and pressed on, staring at her toes as they tried to dig their way into the wide-planked floor. "Samuel was the most insistent. After a couple of weeks, he became agitated, and I panicked. Told them that there was no baby. I thought it was the truth, thought it had to be the truth. My parents were married for years before I came along."

"That's not how it works for everyone, though," Katherine said softly.

"No." Margaretta sighed.

"And Samuel Albany knew that, too," Nash murmured.

His soft words forced Margaretta to look at him, even though she'd been avoiding it. More of that unreadable expression met her gaze, so she let her eyes fall back to her clasped hands.

"Yes. He works a lot with the racing stables, and he kept visiting, saying he had business with Father, but making a point to see me every time. I think he was bribing my maid because he seemed to know almost as soon as I did. He got angry, made veiled remarks about ways he'd heard women got rid of unwanted children. My father and I didn't know what he would do, so Father sent me on a sea-bathing trip with Mrs. Hollybroke and her daughters. Father said he'd join me there in a few weeks."

Margaretta took a deep breath, knowing the next thing she'd done had been foolish. "But Samuel's man followed sooner. I'd been in Margate but three days when I saw him outside the house where we were staying. I got scared. So I ran."

The tears returned. A slow steady trickle down her cheeks that blurred her vision and added to the misery coursing through her.

Strong arms suddenly wrapped around her as Nash pulled her to his chest, making her feel truly safe for the first time in months. She curled into the steady warmth, her body beginning to shake from the overwhelming emotions. For just a moment, part of her believed everything was going to come out right in the end.

Mrs. Lancaster sniffled in the corner, not even bothering to hide the fact that she was crying.

"But why did you come here?" Katherine was standing now, but still looked wary, staying several feet from Margaretta and Nash.

Margaretta straightened within the circle of Nash's arms so she could see her old friend better. "When you left London, there were whispers. They said you were with child, and I couldn't imagine another reason you would have left like that. I had hoped you would know what I could do, where I could go. A way to hide my condition and never let the world know it happened. All I had was the letter you sent me from Marlborough, so I came here. I didn't know what else to do."

The slow stream of tears became a flood as Margaretta finally allowed herself to feel everything. She sobbed into Nash's chest. Tears of freedom from finally sharing her burden with someone else. Tears of hopelessness because it didn't appear that Katherine had found a real solution either. All the tears she'd done her best to hold back for months came pouring out. She cried for John, perhaps the first time since he'd died, and she cried for his family, who mourned ever so much more than she had. Mostly though, she selfishly wept for herself, for the unfairness of life, for the strength she didn't know if she had.

Another set of arms wrapped around Margaretta's shoulders and pulled her away from Nash, toward one of the doors off the main room.

She didn't want to leave his warmth, didn't want to leave him. Desperate for one last look at his face, she tilted her head up as his arms fell away from her. More tears spilled, blurring the lines of his face and preventing her from reading the expression in his deep blue eyes.

She tore her tear-filled gaze from his, unwilling to drag out the breaking of her heart any more than she had to. Would she ever see him again?

Would he tell her father? Did it matter?

Would Katherine be able to give her any answers? She was living alone with Miss Blakemoor and her baby. How were they surviving? Whatever resources they had, Margaretta didn't have access to similar ones.

The room Katherine took her to was warm. Margaretta couldn't see through the tears, and her eyelids were starting to puff and swell from the force of her crying. But she could feel the blessed softness of a mattress and soon the welcoming darkness of oblivion silenced her pain.

A hearty wail broke into Margaretta's slumber. As she blinked awake, she tried to remember where she was, a problem she'd never had until a few weeks ago, having spent most of the first twenty years of her life waking up in her father's London townhouse. She eased her eyes open. The room was dim, too dark to be the rooms above Mrs. Lancaster's store. Plastered walls painted a light yellow surrounded her as she snuggled under the pieced scrap quilt. Low murmurs came through the wall, and the baby who had woken her soon silenced.

Katherine's home. Or Mrs. Lancaster's cottage. Whichever way she wanted to think of it.

The chirping of birds greeted her as she got up and found her clothing draped over a chair in the corner. How heavily had she slept that she hadn't even noticed when Katherine removed her dress and shoes?

The room was small, but comfortable, with a bed, chair, and small washstand. The lone window looked out over a small vegetable garden and let in the morning sun.

Tears threatened again, but her head was already pounding from everything that had happened the day before, and she was so very tired of crying. She took a deep breath and pressed her palms to her eyes until the urge subsided.

A sense of urgency swelled in her throat as she dressed, but she delayed leaving the room. Katherine had been Margaretta's last hope, but what help could she really offer? Even if Katherine knew a way for Margaretta to hide and to then provide for the baby, there was still her father and John's parents to consider. She couldn't disappear like Katherine and Miss Blakemoor had.

She also couldn't just go back to London and hope Samuel would come to his senses. She couldn't even afford to leave this cottage until he was gone from Marlborough.

But one thing was certain: She wasn't going to find any answers in this little room.

Miss Blakemoor was sitting in the rocking chair near the fireplace, feeding the baby, as Margaretta stepped out into the main room. "Good morning."

"Good morning, Miss Blakemoor."

She laughed. "Call me Daphne. There's little reason to stand on ceremony here."

Her gaze dropped to Margaretta's middle before looking down at the baby she held. Her smile never faltered.

Margaretta eased forward and sat in one of the chairs. "Everyone thought it was Katherine who was in a delicate condition. They swore it was her who had been caught with Mr. Maxwell Oswald." With a wince, Margaretta realized she'd never even wondered where Daphne had disappeared to. Neither had anyone else. "I'm afraid no one even considered it was you."

"I know." Daphne's smile turned sad. "They probably didn't even know I was gone. Katherine was ruined in their minds, and I was ruined in real life, so we convinced our fathers to give us our dowry money and we would disappear. Mine wasn't very large, of course, but Katherine's... we figured it would be enough to get us somewhere, to get established until we could find a way to provide for ourselves."

She rose to walk, the baby on her shoulder as she patted his back. "We'd intended to go east and then up the coast, find a little bungalow in a seaside town. But the carriage ride made me ill, and then we met Mrs. Lancaster. We'd intended to only stay until I was feeling up to traveling, but that was nine months ago and we're still here."

They fell silent, and Margaretta tried to find the courage to voice the questions she didn't dare ask. Did the father know? Did they intend to live here forever and raise Benedict themselves? They'd had nine months to think about the future, and Margaretta was deathly afraid that it hadn't been enough time to find a solution because the problem was an impossible one.

"Were you truly married?" Daphne asked quietly, apparently not as petrified as Margaretta was about propriety.

"Yes, I really was. John and I met a few times at parties in the two years I was out in society. Then Father brought him home, proposing the benefits of a connection between our families. I barely knew John, but he seemed nice enough so I agreed."

Silence fell again. Whether or not both women were thinking the same thing, Margaretta couldn't say, but it felt to her like the unspoken question on both of their tongues was *What are you going to do?* Margaretta imagined they both wanted to ask each other the question but each felt she couldn't since she didn't know how to answer it for herself.

A grumble from Margaretta's empty belly broke the silence, prompting her to inquire about food. Each bite she took of her simple breakfast sounded loud in the silent room. Perhaps taking her chances in Mrs. Lancaster's tiny rooms would be better than this, even though being in the center of town greatly increased the chances of Samuel or his man finding her.

The front door opened, and Katherine bustled in with a basket full of fabric. She dropped the basket next to the door and looked from Daphne to Margaretta and back again. "Have you been like this all morning?"

"Kit . . ." Daphne's voice was low.

Katherine rolled her eyes at her friend. "Do you really think proper parlor manners are called for here?" She took off her pelisse and hung it on a hook by the door before moving to sit across from Margaretta. "What are you planning to do?"

Apparently Katherine had no problem voicing the question. She always had been a bit more blunt than most.

Margaretta sighed and put down her tea. "I don't know. I spent days in my room pondering that question, praying in ways I never had before. Then I remembered your letter—"

"You sent letters?" Daphne paused in the act of putting her son down in his cradle. "We agreed to disappear."

Katherine didn't even look ashamed. "I wanted to say good-bye to a few people, let them know I was leaving and not dead in a ditch somewhere. Besides, I didn't think we were going to be staying in Marlborough for more than a day. It seemed like a safe enough place to mail them from."

Daphne dropped into the third chair at the table. "How many?"

Another sigh and another eye roll. Perhaps that was how Katherine expressed herself when she felt backed into a corner. "Only three."

"If it's any consolation, I don't think anyone else will be looking for you." Margaretta hesitated, but perhaps they all needed a bit of Katherine's blunt honesty. "I probably wouldn't have remembered it except that I found myself desperate to know what you'd done if the rumors were true."

"But you're a proper widow." Daphne picked at her fingernails.

"A fact that actually has me in more danger at the moment than the alternative would have."

"But if the child is a girl, you could simply go home." Katherine fixed her own cup of tea from the pot Margaretta had made earlier.

"Yes." That was the best outcome she could hope for. But even then she'd be taking a child home to what? Care and comfort, yes, but Margaretta was now a widow with limited prospects. Could she take the child and live with John's family, knowing the kind of man Samuel was? Would she stay home and wait for her father to marry her off again? What sort of man wanted to marry a woman who came with a daughter?

The idea of marrying again threatened to send Margaretta right back to bed, where she could cry herself into oblivion. Where she had once welcomed the security of an emotionless marriage, it had lost a great deal of its appeal in the past month. She'd learned that relationships could be different, and it was difficult to go back to thinking otherwise.

"Will you take a boy to the foundling house then?" Katherine's question was quiet. So quiet Margaretta wasn't sure she simply hadn't thought it.

Because she'd thought it before. Thought it often.

"I can't." Margaretta's throat seemed to swell. The words she knew she needed to get out felt thick and syrupy as they slid through the thin passage, fighting for space with Margaretta's shallow breaths. "I thought maybe I could, but I can't. I didn't love John, but this child is from a marriage that, however short, happened. I can't leave him on the doorstep, to be scorned and treated like an unwanted blight on the world."

"No child should be left to think that of themselves," Daphne added with a look toward the cradle in the corner. A look that said she loved her son more than anything, more than the tough road she'd been forced to walk to get here, more than the mountains they would still have to climb.

Margaretta looked back and forth between the two women at the table. "How are you going to do it? Mrs. Lancaster isn't going to live forever."

Katherine nodded to the basket she'd dropped by the door. "We take in some sewing. A bit of mending, some work for the church, making clothes for the people in the workhouse. It's all arranged through a local seamstress, a friend of Mrs. Lancaster's. All those years of embroidery mean I can sew a pretty straight stitch. We've enough to purchase a house when it comes time. As long as we make money for food, we should be able to survive, possibly even thrive eventually."

Daphne splayed her fingers across the table and then curled them into fists. "Mrs. Lancaster said that once the baby is weaned, she'd find a way to make sure he was taken care of." Her gaze shifted again to the quiet baby in the corner. "But I can't do it. I can't spend these first months with Ben and then give him up."

Katherine reached a hand over and wrapped her fingers around Daphne's fist in a show of silent support.

There was no way Margaretta could mimic their plan. She hadn't the funds or the help. But another idea crept into her mind. "I could send money."

She winced. That wasn't how she'd meant to broach the idea.

Both women looked at her with raised eyebrows.

Margaretta cleared her throat and forged ahead. What was the worst that could happen? They would say no and kick her out of their house? She'd be no worse off than she was right now, except that she wasn't sure how to get back to Mrs. Lancaster's store. "I'll get pin money. I could send some. To help."

"Help who?" Katherine asked.

"Help you. If the baby is a boy . . . If I left him with you, could you keep him? . . . Could you give him a good home?"

Nine

Nash hadn't slept. Ideas and inclinations had run through his head, distracting him to the point he'd nearly cut himself while shaving. He was drowning in the very thing he'd spent nearly a decade determined to avoid: emotion so crippling that he couldn't live his daily life.

Behind him, his desk was strewn with work, but he hadn't done any of it. Despite the fact that he was considerably behind, he stared out the window.

Not that he saw much beyond the glass. He was too busy remembering the look on Margaretta's face as she'd let her hand trail over his arm while Katherine led her away. She'd been pleading for something, using those bottomless dark eyes to try to rip his soul from his body with the claws of her dripping tears. But Nash had left. Even before Katherine had closed the door to the bedroom, he'd fled the cottage. Nothing would ever be the same for him. Or for her.

Recognition of two of the men walking through the morning hustle and bustle of High Street broke through Nash's ponderings. Mr. Fortescue and Mr. Albany were walking down the street, presumably in the direction of Nash's office. The older man's face was set in determined lines while the younger man curled his lip in distaste. Whether his disdain was for the early hour or the town itself, Nash couldn't tell. Nor did he care. After everything he'd learned over the past twenty-four hours, Nash wasn't inclined to like the man.

In fact, his inclinations veered much closer to running Samuel Albany out of town than ensuring his welcome to the local stables and coaching inns.

There was nothing he could do, however. Nash's opinion of the situation didn't matter. In the eyes of the law, the man had done nothing wrong. If possessing ambition and desiring to inherit a title were criminal offenses, quite a bit of England's aristocracy would be rotting in Newgate.

Margaretta's husband had died nearly four months ago, based on all the information Nash had put together over the past few weeks. That was more than enough time to know if she'd gotten with child during her short marriage, and the fact that she was running, hiding, would only serve as evidence to Samuel Albany if he was, indeed, as crazed and obsessed as Margaretta believed.

As the two men crossed the street, Nash could see that they were arguing, with Mr. Fortescue looking nearly ready to explode into a tirade. Whether that would manifest itself as a physical or verbal assault on the younger man remained to be seen, but it settled some of Nash's fear that Margaretta's father was somehow betraying the safety of his daughter.

The two men stopped outside the door to Nash's office, but his position at the window allowed him to hear their hushed, angry voices.

"One has to wonder how well you can control a business if you can't control your daughter, Mr. Fortescue," Mr. Albany snarled.

The threat didn't seem to do anything to fluster Mr. Fortescue's composure. It was easy to see where Margaretta had gathered the strength to set out on her own.

The older man flung open the door to Nash's office and strolled in. "A business is ever so much more predictable than a woman." He sent an inquisitive look in Nash's direction. "Wouldn't you agree, Mr. Banfield?"

Given that Nash's ability to guess what a woman was about was essentially nil, he had to agree. He nodded. "Of course, sir." The younger man grunted and narrowed his eyes in Nash's direction. "You didn't come to dinner."

Nash turned, maintaining his position by the window. "Urgent business arose with another client. As only a few of the men you requested to speak with were interested and none available until today, I decided to wait until this morning."

"We wish to speak to them all, Mr. Banfield." Mr. Albany's lip curled. "If you can't make that happen, I'll find a solicitor who can."

There were only two other solicitors in Marlborough, one of whom was nearly seventy and wrote simple contracts at a small desk in the corner of his drawing room, so Nash wasn't incredibly worried about the threat. What did concern him was getting Samuel Albany out of reach of Margaretta as quickly as possible. Yes, he felt betrayed that she'd kept such a secret from him, and the discovery left his chest feeling like it had been hollowed out with a cricket bat, but he still wanted to make her happy, keep her safe.

"Perhaps, gentlemen," Nash settled himself into the chair behind his desk and steepled his fingers underneath his chin, "I could be of better service if I knew more about what you were actually looking for."

Mr. Fortescue's eyes narrowed, but Mr. Albany's gaze became hazy and unfocused as he paced across the room to the window. "I intend to make my name known across the country, Mr. Banfield. My grandfather may have started our racing stable, but I intend to bring it into the nineteenth century. We will be the stable that everyone talks about, the one that the Arabian princes come to visit. And I intend to be the one who makes it so."

A fiery passion rode his features as he turned back to Nash and braced his hands against the desk to lean forward. "One day, the Albany racing stables will be mine, and then—" His words broke off, and he hung his head, taking a deep breath as if collecting his thoughts. "The Albany racing stables are an important part of my family legacy, Mr. Banfield, and I *will* be a part of it."

Nash glanced at Mr. Fortescue, noting the paleness of the man's skin behind the determined set of his jaw. Thoughts tumbled over each other in Nash's head, the foremost of which was that Samuel Albany didn't seem to be in complete control of his faculties. He was a man obsessed with power and prestige, none of which he could expect to gain as a third son unless he took it for himself. And that made him dangerous to Margaretta.

A niggling thought tickled Nash's mind, a vague memory prodding an idea. Was there any chance Samuel's passion could be redirected? Was it possible Nash could point him in a direction that would let him make a name now instead of waiting to inherit control of the family stable?

"Passion for a family legacy is admirable." Nash cleared his throat and rose, walking slowly to a stack of magazines on a low table. The article he was remembering was a couple of months old, but if he could find it . . . A copy of *Sporting Magazine* lay at the bottom of the pile, its edges curling around themselves. "Perhaps that could be better found in making a mark on the sport as a whole."

Nash's heart threatened to pound out of his chest as he took the magazine back to his desk and settled into his chair once more. He had to tread very carefully through this conversation. He couldn't give away that he knew anything about Mr. Fortescue's daughter or Mr. Albany's family situation. One word, one slip could be a disaster. The safest thing would have been to remain quiet, but he'd just introduced a suggestion that required he drive the conversation.

Oh well. In for a penny . . . "There's a new style of racing in Ireland."

He plopped the magazine on his desk, open to an article entitled, "A Curious Horse-Race." Mr. Albany scooped up the paper and settled into a nearby chair to read, but Mr. Fortescue remained focused on Nash, his eyes assessing and thoughtful.

Nash swallowed. "I'm not much of a sportsman, gentlemen, but it seems to me that the right leadership could take the idea of this idle wager and turn it into a horse racing empire." That was possibly laying it on too thick, but Nash couldn't back off now.

Mr. Albany looked up. "They had jumps in the race?"

"Yes." Nash looked at Mr. Fortescue out of the corner of his eye. "And if someone were to make a special saddle for just such a race, it would no doubt be to the racer's advantage."

"No doubt," Mr. Fortescue murmured. "It would be quite a coup to be the first to introduce such a novel thing to England's shores. Surely not something an Irishman would be capable of."

Mr. Albany slapped the magazine down onto his leg. "Fortescue Saddles will not take the credit for this. Any saddle you make for this will be for Albany use only."

"Of course." Mr. Fortescue cleared his throat. "But I'd need to study how this racing is done."

Nash shuffled some blank papers on the surface of his desk. "We could draw up an agreement now, if you wish, that any development in saddles made for this new style of jump racing will be for the exclusive use of the Albany stables."

Mr. Albany seemed to preen under the idea of exclusive rights to anything. "Yes. We could even name the saddle after us. It would need to be a priority development."

"Of course." Mr. Fortescue seemed to sink into his chair with a sigh of relief. Perhaps this was the first time he'd relaxed in weeks. How long had he been following this madman around the country?

"We need to take control of this soon," Mr. Albany declared, then paused. "But we cannot neglect our . . . current project."

Mr. Fortescue tightened back up in his seat. "Nothing will change in the time it takes us to travel to Ireland and study this. We can address the issue when we return."

Nash knew the man was hoping that by the time they returned the issue would have settled itself, and Margaretta would have either had a girl or found a safe place to hide the baby if it were a boy. The alternative, that Margaretta or the baby didn't survive the duration of their absence, was probably eating through Nash's thoughts alone. No father would want to consider such an end for his daughter.

"I suppose." Mr. Albany looked back at the article in his lap before nodding at Nash. "Draw up the papers."

<hr />

Margaretta was placing small, neat stitches in the ripped shoulder seam of a rough white shirt when Mrs. Lancaster came through the door around midday. The women were still seated at the table, discussing the possibilities open to Margaretta, though Katherine had declared that they at least needed to do something worthwhile as they talked.

Where Margaretta's cleaning skills were decidedly lacking, her sewing was almost as accomplished as her cooking. She'd already set a pot over the fire to heat a stew for their supper.

Conversations stumbled to a halt as Mrs. Lancaster let herself into the tiny cottage. She beamed at the three of them. "Look at you ladies. Making the most of life when the devil would rather strike you down. I'm proud of you."

Daphne blushed but didn't look away as the old woman came forward to look at the bundle in her arms.

"Ah, such a sweet little one." The shopkeeper looked up and smiled. "And our other sweet little one? Have we settled things there?"

Katherine and Daphne looked at each other for a long moment. While many potential details had been discussed, an actual agreement had yet to be reached. Finally Katherine gave a little nod. "We're keeping Margaretta's baby."

Mrs. Lancaster's smile fell as she looked straight at Margaretta. "You'd leave your baby behind?"

Until that moment, Margaretta hadn't really let herself think of it that way. She'd thought of it more as taking care of someone in need. Like a charity that could be done impersonally with a bit of separation. But at that moment, with the sadness and possibly even disappointment on Mrs. Lancaster's face, her baby became just that. *Hers.*

It didn't change the facts, though. "I haven't a dowry to bring or anything to start my life with. If I go home, marry, seek the life I was born for, I'll have money that I can send back to help. If it's a girl, I might be able to keep her. Otherwise—" she lay her hand over her middle—"it's simply not a risk I can afford to take."

Katherine sighed. "For what it's worth, I think you should tell John's family. I think they would protect you."

"Samuel is the only son they have left living on English soil. I can't take the chance that they'd believe him over me." Margaretta paused so she didn't stab herself with the needle. "And they'll insist I come live with them, under their roof. Hiding from Samuel wouldn't be an option anymore."

It was a great risk she was taking, not telling John's family about the baby. If it turned out to be a boy, if he was in line to inherit, would they believe her when she claimed it was John's? Or was she dooming her child to a life without his birthright?

Mrs. Lancaster came around the table to hug Margaretta tight. "Don't you worry none. God's not surprised by one bit of this. Mark my words, my dear, He's got a plan big enough for everyone. And sometimes"—she pressed a kiss into Margaretta's hair—"those plans are hard to understand."

Margaretta didn't know what to do with the open affection of Mrs. Lancaster, but it felt like a balm on her aching heart. Daphne and Katherine reached their hands across the table and twined fingers with Margaretta. The moment was solemn, like a vow between the women to do the best they could with these lives that they'd been entrusted with for whatever reason. Emotion overwhelmed her, led by fear that they were doing the wrong thing.

These babies needed so much guidance, so much education, so much of everything if they were going to make their ways in this world. Could four ladies who didn't know what they were doing manage it?

It was enough to make her want to slink to her bed and not come out for a week.

Then Benedict peeked around his blanket, blinked at her, and burped.

As the most basic of noises broke the solemn silence, the four women gave into laughter instead of tears, and Margaretta knew that Mrs. Lancaster was right. No matter how lost she felt, none of this was a surprise to God.

Working out the contract took the better part of the day, but by the time evening rolled around, both men were smiling. Well, Mr. Fortescue was smiling. Mr. Albany looked like a smug cat who'd stolen the cream.

Nash promised the men he would make clean copies of the agreement and have it messengered to London, as well as to Newcastle, Ireland, where the men were intending to travel.

Hands were shaken all around, and Mr. Albany made noises about whether or not it was too late to catch the stage. He eventually decided they would wait until morning. Neither Nash nor Mr. Fortescue offered a thought while Mr. Albany discussed this decision with himself. They simply nodded in agreement.

Mr. Fortescue never stopped eyeing Nash with a bit of skepticism before saying quietly, "I'd still like to discuss those travel arrangements some time."

Nash debated how to answer. He knew that traveling to Ireland and abandoning his daughter had to be a difficult prospect for the older man, but he would do it to keep her safe. Mr. Albany currently didn't seem to care about anything, having been convinced that his name would become synonymous with this new style of horse racing within a year. Nash wasn't willing to test that new fascination, though, by speaking in anything other than vague terms with her father.

"I'm sure I can be of service in that area when the time comes."

Mr. Fortescue's eyes narrowed, probably trying to read Nash's hidden meaning. Then his eyes widened as he took in something beyond Nash's shoulder.

Before Nash could turn and see what had garnered the other man's attention, the door opened, allowing a slight breeze into the office along with Mrs. Lancaster. "Good evening, gentlemen."

Nash swallowed, trying to keep himself from panicking as Mrs. Lancaster waltzed right by Mr. Albany with Margaretta's bag held in front of her. She nodded to the men and came around the desk to set the valise on the ground, out of sight. "I don't mean to interrupt. Mr. Banfield simply agreed to help me with my deliveries today. These old bones can't do quite what they used to."

She cackled, seeming completely at ease and ignorant of the tension her presence had created. Thankfully, Mr. Albany seemed equally ignorant.

Mr. Fortescue, on the other hand, was staring at Nash's desk as if he could see the bag sitting on the floor behind it. His gaze turned hard as it finally flicked up to meet Nash's. "This . . . agreement. I trust you've seen to my interests in it? All of my interests?"

Nash considered playing dumb, just in case Mr. Albany was more astute than he thought, but he couldn't do that to the man. Any father who was willing to set aside his normal business and travel all the way to Ireland simply to protect his daughter deserved to know that she was safe. "Of course, sir." Nash swallowed, but there was no moisture left in his mouth. "I'll make sure that everything of yours is protected."

Mr. Albany huffed. "Yes, yes, isn't that what we just spent that past several hours discussing? Now, let's be off. I need to send my man ahead to inquire about passage to Ireland."

Tension Nash hadn't known he was holding seeped from his muscles at the news that Mr. Albany's man would be traveling with them. With one last glance, Mr. Fortescue rose and followed Mr. Albany to the door. He paused at the portal. "Any updates you feel this . . . agreement needs. You'll send me word?"

Nash nodded. "I'll send it express, sir."

Mr. Fortescue looked sad, but he nodded and followed Mr. Albany out into the street.

Nash collapsed into his chair, exhausted.

Mrs. Lancaster smiled. "Well, that seems to have gone well."

A groan escaped Nash's chest as he laid his head back on his chair. "What are you doing here, Mrs. Lancaster?"

"You need to deliver this to Margaretta tonight. I don't think my legs can take the walk up that hill again."

Nash couldn't help the smile that rose to his lips. Mrs. Lancaster could probably walk halfway to Avebury before feeling a twinge, despite her strange shuffling gait. Still, he could never call her a liar. That didn't mean he wanted to deliver the bag, though. He wasn't ready to see Margaretta. Wasn't sure he would ever be.

She was with child. He knew what that meant in such vivid, horrid detail, knew the ultimate risk, the possible devastating outcome. And he didn't want to think about it.

"She needs her things." Mrs. Lancaster frowned, an expression so foreign that her face seemed to crack in order to make the muscles move into the necessary position. "And you're going to take them to her."

Ten

Nash took Margaretta her bag because, well, because he couldn't figure out a way not to. That didn't mean he had to see her, though. He'd left the bag on the stoop and then knocked before running away like a pranking child, fleeing from the cottage as if it contained the plague instead of a baby and an expecting woman.

He'd included a note, though, stating that her father and Samuel Albany were leaving town, their search for her suspended for the time being. The note was light on details and probably raised more questions than it answered. Was part of him hoping she'd seek him out and demand more information?

If so, he was doomed to disappointment. Two weeks passed without a word.

She didn't return to Mrs. Lancaster's shop, either, choosing instead to stay with the other women at the cottage. Cooking, gardening, and sewing were now taking up her days. He knew because his near daily visits to Mrs. Lancaster's shop had continued. Even though he told himself he was better off without Margaretta in his life, he couldn't help wondering how she was, what she was doing.

At first, Mrs. Lancaster had been happy to tell him things, even saying that the women had a plan for Margaretta's baby. As the days passed, though, Mrs. Lancaster's updates turned into frowns and glares.

Yet still, Nash returned day after day because it was the only way he would learn anything. If something important happened, surely Mrs. Lancaster would break her self-imposed silence.

Though he knew he shouldn't care.

Nash stared at the papers in front of him. The same ones that had been spread across his desk for two days now. While it was true that life in the country moved at a slower pace than that of the city, his clients still expected him to actually do the work they paid him for.

He grabbed a quill and set it to paper, intent on writing out the new dowry agreement for Mr. Jacobson's daughter. It was a straightforward sort of thing, a sum of money determined by her parents' marriage contract. It shouldn't have taken Nash more than an hour to complete it.

Yet here he was, taking the better part of the morning to even set quill to paper.

He was two lines in before he realized he'd never dipped the nib into the inkwell.

Throwing the quill down on the scratched but blank sheet of paper, Nash shoved away from his desk and stalked across the room. Looking back at his desk, he was haunted by the knee hole and drawers facing him.

You've a partner desk but no partner.

While it didn't make sense for him to have a partner here in his little Wiltshire solicitor's office, the statement seemed to echo around the empty halls of the rest of his life as well. He didn't have a partner. Didn't have anyone, really. Even the townspeople who he claimed to feel so beholden to, so protective of, he kept at arm's length.

But still he cared, knowing that one day death would knock on the door of those he'd become accustomed to seeing. Mrs. Lancaster would follow Mr. Lancaster to heaven eventually. Henry Milbank would be replaced by a younger, stronger person when he could no longer handle delivering coal to the businesses in town. Already the man was slowing down and talking of taking on an apprentice.

Because he had no son to train. Life had left Mr. Milbank scarred, and he'd never tried again.

But at least he'd tried. Like Lewis and Mary. Nash couldn't claim such a feat.

Nash had walked away from life, thinking he could limit his involvement and therefore limit his hurt. Just as he'd walked away from Margaretta. He couldn't let her in, couldn't give her his heart, only to have to bury it alongside her should she suffer the same fate as his sister.

The idea that Margaretta might not survive the birth of her child rocked through Nash, sending him to his knees. He groped his way to a chair and pulled himself into it before dropping his head into his hands and taking great, gulping gasps of air into his lungs. The air rushed in and out of his heaving chest until his lips begin to tingle.

It was too late.

If Margaretta died, he would be crushed. Even the idea that she would suffer pain caused tears to spring to his eyes. And what if she lived? Would she change her mind and keep the child? Would she stay here? She had no money, no job, no place to live unless she stayed with her friends who, from all appearances, were already on limited funds.

Nash knew, from all the contracts and documents he'd written over the years that her choices were more than limited. They were nonexistent. She would have to marry.

And she would marry someone who wasn't Nash.

Because he had walked away from her. Did she ask Mrs. Lancaster about him? Did she feel betrayed by his absence? She had to feel like he'd rejected her. After all, he hadn't been to see her once since her secret had been revealed. It was likely that she had—quite accurately—guessed that he was unable to handle her situation.

But could he? If he could take back the past two weeks, if he could go back and assure her that the feelings that had grown unacknowledged between them were true and real, would he? Was there a way back from his quiet rejection?

More than that, could he take the risk? He hadn't fathered the child, but he could be the one to suffer if there were consequences. Did it matter?

The door to his office clicked open, and he made himself stand to greet whoever came in. There was still a business to be run, after all, and it was distinctly possible that this business would soon be all he had.

Margaretta rubbed the side of her growing middle. It seemed in the past week she'd gone from slightly rounded to obviously enlarged. It was enough to keep her inside no matter how badly she wanted more space to breathe fresh air. Marlborough was currently filled with England's elite on their way to their summer abodes. She couldn't risk word of her location or condition getting back to Samuel, even in Ireland.

For now she'd have to content herself with circling the small room in Mrs. Lancaster's cottage.

A sudden lurch against her hand brought her stumbling to a halt. Was that . . . could it be?

With one hand braced against the wall to steady her suddenly weak knees, Margaretta took her other hand and pressed it hard against the place that had just fluttered.

There it was again.

The briefest shift, barely anything and not much different that the other minor aches and pains she'd been experiencing, except that she knew it was different. She knew it was her baby.

There was a baby inside her, a living thing, and no longer was it something she knew, like she knew her sums and who the King of England was. This was real. She was growing a brand-new human being. A child who would one day run and laugh like the neighborhood children.

A son who would have to learn to grow up and be a man with someone else leading the way.

Or a daughter who would have to be equally as strong as she grew up without a clear sense of belonging or purpose, bearing a dead man's name, assuming John's parents would even acknowledge her after Margaretta had claimed to be without child. They had no real motivation to claim her. For most, a daughter was simply a bargaining tool to be married off for social or economic gain.

Margaretta slid to the floor and wrapped her arms around her middle, praying it was a son. She knew she'd have to leave him behind if it was, but Mrs. Lancaster had assured her that he would be taken care of in this small town. It'd be a simple life, not worthy of his father's lineage, but he'd be safe, perhaps even loved.

Leaving him would be in the name of survival, but Margaretta wasn't sure she would survive it. It would difficult, but at least she'd know. She wouldn't have to wonder every day for the rest of her life if he was well. Which would be worse? To watch her daughter struggle to find her place in life, trapped between her mother's rich merchant upbringing and her father's younger child aristocracy, or miss out on the smiles and hugs with her son?

She'd seen Daphne cooing and laughing with her own son, had cheered along with Katherine when Benedict picked his head up all by himself and waved his little fist in the air.

Margaretta's trembling hand ran over her belly once more. There was every chance she wouldn't be a part of cheering for this little one.

Salty tears pooled against Margaretta's lips as she leaned her head back against the wall. Mindlessly, she swiped at her face, almost surprised that her hand came away wet. Was she crying for the child or for herself? Did it matter? With that single flutter, everything had changed. Margaretta would never be able to completely separate herself from this baby ever again. Not in her heart, anyway.

Just as she knew that even if she married again, it would be as practical as her first marriage.

Fresh tears streamed down her cheeks. It hadn't mattered that she'd told herself not to fall in love with the solicitor, that a life with him was as likely as a life in which she got to keep her child.

It wasn't fair. She wanted to scream at God and yell at the ceiling. She'd done everything right. She'd been the perfect model of what a young English girl should be, seeking to advance her father's position by aligning with a family higher on the social ladder, even if he was a second son with very few prospects.

She'd done everything right. So why was her life falling apart now?

Nash stopped at the end of the alley, looking at the boys playing on the green, remembering an evening not too many weeks ago when he'd watched a similar scene, unaware of the fact that everything he thought he knew about life and himself was about to change.

Three boys ended up in a pile on top of each other, laughing and squealing while the other four boys circled around them and cheered.

Would Margaretta's son play on this field one day? Would there be a child with pale skin and dark hair lining up with the other neighborhood children on market day, hoping that the sweets vendor decided to give them the broken candies for free?

This was assuming, of course, that mother and child even survived the birthing process.

Richard, the fourth son of an innkeeper, broke away from the pack, spinning some sort of cloth over his head. Jeremiah, the eldest son of the town banker, ran after him. The chances of the boys remaining friends when they were too old to run around on the green were slim, but the future wasn't stopping them from enjoying life right now. Neither was the past.

There was something to be learned from that. Perhaps that was what Jesus meant when he said, "Take therefore no thought for the morrow: for the morrow shall take thought for the things of itself." Perhaps that was what living for today was, because there was certainly enough right here and right now for him to concern himself with. And if he were living for today, why was he doing things to make his day so miserable?

He nearly ran the rest of the way across the green and down the street to the little cottage. Was he really going to do this? Go through that door and do everything he'd vowed to never do?

Yes, he was. Because he already loved her.

The only question was whether or not he'd spend whatever was left of their lives together showing her how much. A smile graced his face for the first time in weeks, free because he'd finally decided to let go of that fear and hold on to the joy they seemed to bring each other.

His knock went unanswered, so he pushed open the door, worry nibbling away at the fragile hope he'd just found. With three women doing their best to be forgotten by the world, shouldn't at least one of them be home?

The door creaked on its hinges as he pushed it open.

He winced, hoping Benedict wasn't sleeping in the main room.

The baby was the last thing on his mind, though, when he saw Margaretta huddled in a ball against the wall.

"Margaretta?" He half ran, half slid his way across the room until he was on his knees at her side. "My love, what's wrong?"

"Don't—" she took a deep shuddering breath—"Don't call me that. I don't want to remember you calling me that."

He cupped her face and slid a thumb along her cheek to catch a tear. "I want you to hear it. I want you to know it. Because it's true. You are my love, and I'm so very sorry that you've had to live these past weeks without knowing that."

Her answer was a shaky, trembling wail that shot to his heart, breaking down the last part of the wall he'd built to try to protect himself. He settled onto the floor next to her and scooped her into his lap. She felt so right in his arms, making him feel whole when he hadn't even known he was missing anything. As she cried into his shoulder, he held her, rubbing a soothing hand across her back or over the curls that that had escaped her bun.

A shot of guilt niggled at the back of his mind. He didn't have the right to hold her like this, not until he knew she was in agreement with the direction his mind was rapidly taking. It was as if the moment he'd given himself permission to feel again, to join life again, he'd surged toward the one thing he wanted more than anything else.

Margaretta.

Already part of his mind was filled with thoughts of marriage, debating which church to read the banns in since she didn't really live in the town. Perhaps he should take the stage into London and see about getting a special license so they could avoid the complications altogether and just marry quietly.

He leaned his head back against the wall and tried not to laugh at himself. When he changed his mind, he did it wholeheartedly, didn't he?

A final sob escaped Margaretta, and she sat up in his lap, wiping furiously at her tearstained face. It was splotchy and a bit swollen, but he didn't care. To him, it was beautiful, because it meant she was letting him in, letting him see her vulnerabilities and inner fears. It meant something when a woman let a man see her cry.

"You don't mean that," she whispered.

"Yes." Nash swallowed. "I do."

She placed a hand on the middle of her belly and looked down. Curled up as she was, it was impossible to see the slight bump he knew was there, the curve that her loose skirts could almost hide until the wind pressed them against her body. Was she thinking his love didn't extend to that part of her? To the baby she created with another man, a man he knew she hadn't loved?

Nash covered her hand with his. "I love your child, too. Our child. Or at least he can be." The breath Nash pulled into his lungs made him shudder. "If you marry me, I can have you both—love you both. Show you that every day is made for living, just as God has showed me."

Watery brown eyes rose to meet his.

"I haven't been living," Nash whispered. "I've been hiding from life, thinking that staying safe was the way not to hurt, but it was only a way to die before death actually came calling. I don't want to be like that anymore. I want to live, with every breath God has left to give me. I want to live, and I want as many of those breaths as possible to be shared with you."

Something he thought was hope rippled through her eyes, only to be dimmed once more. She caught her lip between her teeth. "Samuel—"

"Has nothing to do with us. I'll claim this baby as mine, and the world won't be able to say differently unless we admit it."

If it was a boy, there might be complications, guilt that they were possibly keeping him from a greater purpose in life. But were titles more important than love and safety? Was there anything being the potential heir presumptive could bring this child that Nash couldn't provide, aside from a position at the edge of the aristocracy?

He took a deep breath, knowing that he'd let Margaretta decide. If she wanted, they would go to her late husband's family and tell them everything; but if she didn't, he would gladly raise this child as his own.

Nash began to talk. He drew a picture in her mind of what their life could be. Of the way he'd imagined this child—their child—playing with the other children in the town, looking forward to market day and growing up to become a solicitor or a soldier or anything else he wanted to become. He talked about sneaking the child peppermints from Mrs. Lancaster's store while Margaretta pretended to glare at him for spoiling the children.

With every sentence he felt her relax, settle deeper into his embrace. Occasionally she chuckled. Eventually her arms unwrapped from around her middle and eased their way around him, bringing her fully into his embrace.

Where she belonged.

Nash took a deep breath. "Marry me, Margaretta. Stay here. Love me. Let's build this life together." In answer, she leaned forward and pressed her lips to his. He could taste the salt of her tears, feel the trembling of her body.

A soft click sounded through the room, but it took him more than a moment to realize what it meant.

"Well, I hope this means you're getting married." Katherine leaned back against the door and crossed her arms over her chest, a frown on her face.

Beside her, Miss Brightmoor was grinning from ear to ear while she snuggled a wrapped baby to her chest. "Of course they are. They love each other."

One side of Katherine's mouth lifted. "I guess they do, don't they."

Epilogue

Two months later, Nash was sitting down at the dining table in the house he'd leased for himself and Margaretta, just a little ways down the road from Mrs. Lancaster's cottage. He'd received a letter from Margaretta's father that morning, letting them know that he and Samuel Albany were engrossed in designing and testing a new saddle, one that would be perfect for the new style of racing. The idea wasn't quite taking off yet, but Samuel had found a new obsession and was determined to bring the style into the sport.

Nash wished him every bit of luck as long as it kept his focus off Margaretta.

A smile touched Nash's lips as his wife maneuvered around her extended belly to serve dinner to their friends. Katherine and Daphne had taken to bringing little Benedict by and spending the evening with Margaretta at least three times a week. Sometimes Mrs. Lancaster joined in.

Usually the evening was loud and joyful, but tonight Daphne seemed subdued. Her spoon scraped against her plate as she pushed the food around instead of eating it.

Margaretta set aside her own spoon and frowned. "What's wrong, Daphne?"

Daphne looked up, her sweet round face pinched and serious. "I was just wishing that everyone had a Nash. You're so fortunate, Margaretta, so blessed."

Heat crawled up Nash's cheeks as everyone took turns glancing from him to the cradle Benedict was currently sleeping in. It wasn't hard to tell where Daphne's sadness had come from. While the two girls had been incredibly happy for Margaretta, there was no running from the fact that no one had come to Daphne's rescue.

Katherine reached a hand across the table and wrapped her fingers around Daphne's. "We'll do it. We'll be someone's Nash."

Margaretta's wide eyes met Nash's. "What do you mean?"

"Well, we were willing to raise your child for you, but now we don't have to." Katherine swallowed and squared her shoulders as if the idea she was proposing scared her even as she was determined to do it. "So we'll do it for someone else. We all know there are more girls out there facing this impossible position."

"But we can't help them all," Daphne said quietly.

"No," Katherine answered. "But we can help one. And maybe . . . maybe that's enough."

The group around the table fell silent.

An idea formed in the back of Nash's mind. It was possibly unscrupulous, and definitely not what his client had in mind, but Nash couldn't deny that the solution seemed like a perfect one. One that might have been created by God himself. Still, he couldn't bring himself to do more than whisper, "What if you could help more than one?"

Three sets of eyes swung his way.

"We can barely support ourselves, Nash," Daphne said just as quietly. "Taking in even one more is going to be difficult enough."

Nash swallowed. "What if we could fix that?"

The sun was starting to crawl down the sky by the time Nash had borrowed his neighbor's horse and wagon and convinced Mrs. Lancaster to watch Benedict. There should still be enough time to show the women what he meant, which was good because he didn't think he could find the words to explain it. Partly because he still couldn't believe what he was suggesting.

As he drove the wagon down a rutted road leading out of Marlborough, Nash wasn't sure which was pounding more, his brain or his heart. What he was about to propose went against every cautious bone in his body. If he did this, if they did this, what would it mean for their lives? He glanced at Margaretta, snuggled up against him.

But what would it mean for so many other lives? For the women like Margaretta who had no way of supporting themselves, much less a child? Women who were forced to consider extreme measures to ensure survival?

Visions of what Margaretta would have done if he hadn't followed her into Mrs. Lancaster's shop that first day tried to crowd his mind. Nausea rolled through his stomach as he thought about what might have been. What would have happened if she'd been forced to return home and face Samuel. What would have happened if she'd chosen not to return home at all.

He shook his head and guided the horses onto an overgrown lane, branches and vines dragging against his head.

None of the things he was picturing had happened. None of them would happen. Margaretta was safe at his side, and just that morning he'd felt his child kicking away.

The women giggled and pushed through the trees that fell toward the wagon. This property hadn't been in Nash's care long, and clearing the drive hadn't been his top priority, especially since the solicitor who contacted him about finding a caretaker hadn't bothered making arrangements for the property, even though his client had owned it for years.

Nash saw no reason why the caretaker couldn't be a couple of women and a handful of children. There were a few men in the town who would support such an endeavor, see to the more laborious tasks. And with the neglect and overgrowth of the surrounding lands, no one even had to know they were here.

They broke through the overgrown brush and pulled up in front of an estate house that hadn't seen residents in well over a decade.

The giggles subsided.

Katherine leapt from the wagon bed as it rocked to a stop. "Nash, this place is enormous."

It was. Giant two-story columns rose from the front porch, flanked by two large sets of stairs climbing to the house's double doors. Two wings stretched out from the central section and a third stretched backward, though the women couldn't see that yet.

"It needs a caretaker. I've been charged with setting up a long-term solution."

Katherine looked from the house to Nash and back again. Then her gaze swung to Daphne. "What do you think?"

Daphne pressed a hand to her mouth and looked at Margaretta, then back to Katherine. "I think I'd have been in even more dire straits than Margaretta if you hadn't saved me. I'd like to pass that on."

Margaretta wrapped her arms around Nash's arm. "And you won't be alone." She looked at Nash. "None of us will be."

Katherine blew out a breath. "There's things we'll have to consider. The caretaker's funds won't support a passel of children. We'll have to decide what we can actually handle and how to know who to help." She looked around the property again. "But if you want to do it, then I'm in agreement."

Nash couldn't look away from Margaretta as a feeling of purpose swelled in his chest alongside the love that threatened to explode out of him now. "We'll figure it all out. Together."

"Together," Margaretta whispered back.

Nash smiled before he leaned in to give her a quick kiss. Living again felt wonderful.

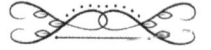

What happens next?

Pick up the story twelve years later with Katherine's story in the first book of the Haven Manor series, *A Defense of Honor*.

Saving Miss Caulfield

Saving Miss Caulfield

If Miss Bianca Caulfield laughed at one more thing her idiot of a dancing partner said, Landon Sinclair was going to break something.

Preferably Mr. Camden Theodore's toes.

Then the cad wouldn't be able to whisk her away from the protection of her mother and brother under the guise of an innocent quadrille in a London ballroom. What were they thinking, letting him court Bianca?

He supposed he should call her Miss Caulfield now, but she had always been Bianca to him.

She was easy to spot in the crush of dancers, her blonde hair twisted into the simplest coiffure in the room. Landon caught glimpses of her light green dress as she moved between the other dancers. She was light on her feet, floating through the complicated dance steps without any effort. It was a hard-won grace, Landon knew. He'd spent hours this winter having his feet trampled and his shins kicked as she tried to learn the steps. Her brother had sported similar injuries, but one would never know it to see her now.

It would have been a pleasure to watch if she weren't smiling up at Mr. Theodore.

"Please tell me you intend to start a mill with that fist, Lord Braidstone. This evening could use a good distraction."

Landon looked down at his hand, surprised to find it curled into a tight ball. With conscious effort he loosened his fingers, stretching them until the knuckles popped. A deep, fortifying breath brought the strong scents of perfume, smoke, and champagne, further reminding him of the conduct expected of a viscount at a social gathering.

He glanced at the speaker, finding the expected grin on his friend's face. "You let her dance with that shuffler, Caulfield?"

Mr. Giles Caulfield, Bianca's brother, shrugged and adjusted his coat sleeve. "Why not? He's well off, popular, and set to inherit a barony."

"He's a pompous windbag who lies his way through what should be gentlemen's dealings and falls asleep in church." Landon made a point of leaning casually against the wall, crossing his arms to hide any fist-making tendencies he might unconsciously entertain.

Giles adjusted his other sleeve. "Pompous or not, his attention has chased off all other interested beau." He cleared his throat and tugged at the first sleeve again. Obviously the man needed a new tailor. Or perhaps his valet had ruined the coat somehow. "Unless you know of someone?"

Landon cast his eyes about the ballroom. There had to be someone better than Theodore. Anyone was better than Theodore. He would trample on Bianca's open heart and sweet spirit, breaking the girl Landon had watched grow up. The mere thought of losing the light of her smile made Landon desperate.

"What about Mr. Bertram?" Landon nodded towards the mill owner across the room. A bit old, perhaps, but he was honorable and loyal and able to provide a good life for Bianca.

Giles shook his head. "Too busy with rebuilding after the Luddites smashed his looms. He's only in Town to visit Parliament."

True enough. Rumor was he'd let his house fall into disrepair as he tried to save his business. Bianca shouldn't live in a rundown house. Landon blew his breath out through pursed lips as he continued his visual search.

That one's reputation was awful. Another given to drunken routs.

His eyes lit on a tall gentleman entering the ballroom. "Fellbourne?"

Giles shook his head. "Has plans to ask for Presbrook's daughter."

The girl who's dinner conversation was limited to the fit of her slippers? Fellbourne never had possessed high enough standards to appreciate Bianca. "Milton?"

"Debt. He'll probably be run out of Town within the month."

Landon jerked his gaze back to Giles. "Truly? I had no idea."

Giles nodded. "I overheard several shopkeepers today while I was waiting for Bianca outside the milliner."

"That won't run him out of town unless he runs up an account at one of the finer establishments. Still, it's a vice Bianca need not deal with." Landon returned to scrutinizing the options in front of him, looking for someone ideal and realistic.

"Miss Caulfield."

What was Giles saying? Bianca was still dancing with that rascal. "Beg your pardon?"

"Bianca. You should call her Miss Caulfield now. At least in public."

Landon grunted in agreement. For propriety's sake he should use a more formal address, but there was a much more pressing issue at stake than adjusting his life-long habits.

The dance set was drawing to a close. Soon Bianca would be back at her mother's side where someone more suitable could ask her to dance. Landon glanced to his left to see if Mrs. Caulfield was still in her previous location. One of Theodore's friends hovered at her elbow.

"It appears that Theodore is determined that your sister not have any other options." Landon nodded his head in Mrs. Caulfield's direction.

Giles gave no more than a glance to the man waiting with his mother. "I believe I mentioned that."

Landon waited, but it became painfully obvious that Giles was going to do nothing to stop Theodore and his cronies from monopolizing Bianca's attention. With a sigh Landon made his way through the crowd along the side of the ballroom.

Giles was a dear friend, closer than any of Landon's own brothers or cousins, but lately he'd been shirking in his brotherly duties towards his sister, leaving Landon to pick up the pieces. They were going to have to talk soon, but first Landon had to save Bianca.

Bianca's face hurt. She'd only been at the ball for an hour and already she was faking the smiles and relying on well-practiced laughter to give the impression of a young woman having the time of her life. In reality she was desperate and growing moreso as the season continued. She couldn't return home without a secure future.

In truth she couldn't return home at all. Mother and Giles tried to assure her that Father wouldn't mind, but they all knew the truth. He'd grumbled for months about the expense of a London season, the uselessness of daughters, and even the size of her dowry, although none of that came directly from him.

God bless her grandfather who had left her a decent dowry when he died. Without it, who knows what her father would have set aside for her?

Mr. Camden Theodore was saying something about country estates and the seclusion from Town, but Bianca could barely make out the words over the pounding of her heart and the constant litany of dance steps running through her mind.

They couldn't afford much time with a dance master, so Bianca had been left to practice with her brother and their generous neighbor, Lord Braidstone.

Landon.

Bianca swallowed a sigh as she kicked her skirt clear of the next intricate step. She strained her ears to hear the music over the loud talking around her and the fears screaming in her mind.

She brought her thoughts back to Landon. He always had a calming effect on her. Such a mixed blessing. He'd been part of every significant moment in her life, another older brother ready to tease her one moment and rescue her the next.

But he'd ruined any chance she had for marital bliss.

The dance ended and Bianca dropped into a curtsy, looking up at Mr. Theodore through her lashes. She tried to picture him as her husband, but the effort was futile. She couldn't imagine a cozy dinner at home with his flat eyes across the table or a quiet stroll through the countryside with his constant stream of boasts and gossip as the only conversation.

That may be her life, though.

"Don't you agree?" he asked with a pat of her hand as he led her from the dance floor.

Bianca smiled. Was the panic reaching her eyes? Because she had no idea what to say and couldn't blindly agree to a question, not when it was entirely possible he'd asked something crucial to her future happiness. The man spoke often of expediency and efficiency. He might have asked her to marry him on the dance floor to save him a trip to her house.

How to get out of this? "I am parched. Do you think they have lemonade?"

His face screwed up in a frown, the only expression that ever reached his eyes. "Of course. You had a glass before we danced. We missed the first song if you'll remember."

A delaying tactic that had caused her to spend more time in his company instead of less. "I had forgotten. It must be the heat. Quite a crush tonight, is it not?"

They reached her mother and Bianca gracefully slid her hand from his elbow, restraining the urge to wipe her glove on her gown. She didn't want to mar the precious light green silk.

"I am sure that Mr. Julian can see to –" His frown darkened. "What are you doing here?"

Bianca spun her head so fast her neck twinged in protest. Mr. Theodore had obviously been expecting his friend, Mr. Julian, to be waiting to claim her for the next dance. Joy, relief, trepidation, and speculation warred for prominence in Bianca's midsection as she took in the welcome sight of Landon's tall form standing beside her beaming mother.

Landon raised his brows and looked around as if wondering what wasn't painfully obvious about his intentions. His brown eyes smiled at her as he brought his gaze back to her. "I'm here to claim Miss Caulfield for the next set."

"But Julian –" Mr. Theodore stumbled to a halt.

Mother waved her hand in the air. "Mr. Julian was here, but I sent him to fetch me a glass of lemonade. It is so dreadfully warm in this crush, isn't it?"

Bianca tried to contain her giggle, but it escaped in an inelegant sputter through her lips. She coughed to hide the embarrassing sound, but ended up sounding like a sick cow as the cough and giggle mingled in her throat.

Landon grinned. "Are you well?"

"Yes, quite." Bianca forced her lips to curve. Hopefully it looked like a smile. Ice. Brisk breezes. Swimming in the lake at the first sign of Spring. She willed the chilly thoughts to keep the heat of a blush away. Her neck grew warm, but her cheeks remained mercifully cool.

"Shall we?" Landon offered his arm.

Bianca pinched herself as she placed her hand on his elbow. She'd danced countless times with him at home, but never had he asked her at an actual event. He claimed she should keep her dances free for the men vying for her hand and attentions.

Oh how it hurt that he didn't number himself among those men.

The music started and they bowed to each other. It was a simple dance, one she'd done since she was a girl, which allowed her to focus on her partner.

Her handsome, kind, intelligent partner.

He leaned his head down as they stepped between the other couples. "I've heard the singer at Vauxhall is quite good."

Bianca felt a blush threaten her ears. What would he do if she ran her fingers through his dark hair? "I haven't had the pleasure of hearing her yet."

"Perhaps we should go then."

They circled around the other couples in their group until they made it to the end of the line, where they stood facing each other. Bianca was floating. Did he actually want to escort her to Vauxhall? Was he finally seeing her as something other than a younger sister? Her prayers must be working.

Landon smiled across the way at her. "What do you think? Shall we make a party? I'm sure your brother would like to go. Is there someone special you would like me to invite?"

Bianca blanched. He couldn't mean what she thought he meant. "Special?"

"Yes." He stepped forward and grasped her hand as they reentered the dance. "Please, anyone but Mr. Theodore. I can't abide the fellow."

Bianca tripped over a simple step and stumbled into Landon's side.

"Oh!" she cried as she righted herself, only to find herself adjusting too much and crashing into the woman on her right.

Landon gripped her arm and righted her with a small laugh. "We'll simply focus on the dancing for now, hmm? Just like old times."

"Just like old times," she said with another cheek torturing smile.

He gave her a brilliant smile as the dance concluded, congratulating her as he always did. And Bianca's heart broke.

The next morning Bianca doodled nonsense on a piece of writing paper, staring out the drawing room window. The Season was nearly half over. Announcements appeared almost daily in the Times. Mother tried not to look worried, but occasionally Bianca found the paper with a name or two circled and she knew another man her mother had hoped to match her with had found someone else.

She was starting to get desperate. Was she to be forced to settle for the first available option? In truth it appeared she was only to have one option. And did it really matter? The man she loved didn't love her and didn't see her as marriage material. Only time, God's grace, and determination were going to make her love her husband. Even then she doubted it would be a passionate love like the couple in Song of Solomon.

At least half of what she'd read in that book of the Bible was beyond her understanding, but it had sounded wildly thrilling and made her think constantly of Landon.

"Lord Braidstone to see you, miss."

Bianca's gaze flew to the maid. Landon never called for her.

And then he was there, his large frame filling the doorway, his brown eyes twinkling and a small smile on his lips. His chestnut hair curled where his hat had been and her fingers itched to smooth it down.

"Good morning." He entered the room and sat in the chair beside her writing desk.

"What are you doing here?" The abruptness of her question made Bianca wince.

"I came to finish our conversation. Giles said you have no fixed engagements for this evening so it seemed a fine time to go to Vauxhall."

Oh yes, the trip to the Gardens. His curiosity about whether or not she had someone special to invite. "Yes. That would be a fine idea."

"Have you thought of anyone we should include in the party?" He settled further back in his chair. "Anyone but Mr. Theodore."

What was wrong with Mr. Theodore? Other than his obvious similarity to all of the other unappealing obsessively ambitious young men she'd met in London. "I'm afraid he's the only one."

He surged from the chair and began to pace. "You cannot seriously be contemplating marriage to that man. He's cruel. I've seen it with my own eyes. He cares nothing for his horses, works his staff to the bone, and neglects any and all things Godly. More often than not he leaves the club foxed. You cannot marry him."

Bianca stood with a frown, resignation pooling in her heart. "Which makes him very similar to half the other men I've met in London. He hasn't asked yet, but he is the only one who potentially will. I hope he does. I don't have any other choice."

"You could go home."

Bianca smiled sadly into Landon's eyes. The hesitant way he'd said the sentence proved he knew how harsh Father's welcome would be if she returned home unwed. He'd declare her a failure and doom her to a miserable secluded spinsterhood.

"Well, there must be someone."

Her hand looked small as she touched his arm to stop his pacing. Her broken heart reached out to him. A pseudo-brother with no acceptable means of aiding her. It must be a difficult position for him.

"There's no one else. If Mr. Theodore asks, I will have to consent. He has an estate in the country. I believe he would be content to leave it for me to run in his absence. With the title, he'll require children. I would be happy to have children."

Landon's frowned darkened. He wrapped his hands around her upper arms and looked deep into her eyes. "You can't marry him."

He crossed to the window, muttering quietly to himself. Was he naming and excusing other men? She didn't even recognize some of the names. Shame coursed through Bianca until it weakened her legs and she fell back into her seat. Even Landon, with all of his connections and social status couldn't think of a decent man who would be interested in marrying her.

"I have no other options." Bianca smiled at him as best she could, but she'd never been able to hide from Landon. He would see her sadness, feel her resignation, and there was nothing she could do about it.

"Yes you do." He spun from the window, his mouth pressed into a line of resolve. "You can marry me."

Bianca stomped through the main hall, wishing she had on something more substantial than satin slippers. Their soft slapping against the marble floor was decidedly unsatisfactory.

She heard Landon exit the drawing room behind her, his boots thudding against the floor with confident solidity. One more grievance for her to lay at his feet.

The urge to run up the stairs was strong, but she forced herself to take the steps at a sedate pace.

"Are you going to answer me?" Landon stood in the hall with his hands on his hips and his head dropped back to look up at her.

Arrogant man. Did he expect her to be delighted about his willingness to sacrifice himself because he couldn't imagine foisting her off on some other poor bloke?

Bianca did her best to arrange her features into a mirror of his frustrated countenance "Are you going to ask me a question?"

She gripped the banister until her fingers turned white and her arm started to shake. Of all the times she had imagined Landon speaking of marriage between the two of them, not once had he suggested it in the guise of a martyr, with a resigned sigh punctuating the moment instead of a passionate kiss.

He shook his head. "Is that what has your dander up? Come back down then, and I'll ask properly. Would you like me on one knee perhaps?"

A noise gurgled in the back of her throat, begging, threatening to escape. A growl? A scream? A cry? Some terrifying combination of the three? She swallowed it down and continued her trek up the stairs, pounding each step with enough force to jar her knees and echo through the house.

Quick, light taps indicated Landon was running up the stairs behind her. She would have to abandon pique to obtain speed if she wished to attain privacy before he reached her.

Her brother, Giles, stood in the corridor at the top of the stairs, blocking the way to the private salon.

"Step aside, please." She made to go around him, but he dodged, placing himself in her path once more. Bianca's eyes narrowed. "Step. Aside. Please."

"No."

Had he truly just denied her retreat? His eyes left her face to look over her shoulder. No doubt Landon had reached them.

Giles cleared his throat and looked between the two of them. "May I ask what brings you visiting so early in the day?"

"I asked your sister to marry me," Landon growled. "Then she left the room."

Bianca's laugh was short and rude. "You did not ask."

He stepped forward, a ruddy splash along his cheekbones matching the angry heat in his gaze. "Will you marry me?"

"No!" Bianca shoved past the two men, fighting the tears. She didn't want a miserable marriage with Theodore, but she didn't want to be pitied either.

How could she possibly have a real marriage with Landon when he saw her as a little sister? Would there even be children? How could she be expected to move past her adoration and love for him if she saw his name every time she signed her own?

If her marriage was doomed to be an arrangement for survival, then she would make it one she had a hope of surviving. Marriage to Landon when he didn't love her back would destroy her.

A strong hand wrapped around her arm and pulled her to a stop. Her momentum swung her around until she faced her captor.

Landon's face was set, the lines around his mouth deepening as his lips flattened. "Earlier you were resigned to a fate with that cad, Theodore. Give me one good reason why you'd choose him over me."

Bianca stared at Landon, blinking slowly. Landon sucked his breath in through his teeth, breathing unaccountably fast.

Giles waved a hand at the door next to him. "I'll be in my study. With the door open."

Landon didn't even glance back as Giles departed. Bianca frowned.

"One reason, Bianca."

What could she say? She could hardly tell him it was because he didn't love her because she was under no illusion that Mr. Theodore loved her either. Telling Landon that she was in love with him would only make him pity her more. She opened her mouth, praying inspiration would strike if she started speaking. "You're... That is to say..."

He leaned back, crossing his arms over his chest with a look of confidence. Was he convinced she couldn't come up with a reason?

"You're too tall." She wanted to crawl under a table. Too tall? That's what she came up with? She deserved his pity for that lack of creativity.

He blinked. "Too tall?"

Her eyes fell to the left. His boot made a fascinating contrast with the polished wood floor.

Then he advanced and her gaze shot back to his face in apprehension. "Too tall? You'll have to come up with something better than that, Bianca. You're too smart to throw away your future on something so meaningless."

Bianca felt her nails cut into her palms as she curled her fingers into fists of determination. He would not pressure her. "Why would I want to marry a man I have to break my neck to look at?"

"Better than a man you'd have to break your soul to live with."

"My soul is stronger than you think, and it's much easier to protect than my heart."

He scoffed. "You think Theodore will have a care for your heart?"

It was Bianca's turn to look superior. "Of course not. But he'll get nowhere near it so it's hardly in danger."

He leaned forward until his breath bounced off her face. "Why would you marry a man who at best will ignore you?"

"Why would I marry a man who pities me?" Bianca's eyes widened and she resisted the urge to clap her hands over her mouth. She hadn't meant to reveal that insecurity, but now that it was out she felt better. There had always been honesty between them.

"I don't pity you." His voice was quiet, barely above a whisper.

"Are you saying you want to marry me because you love me?"

His mouth opened, but nothing came out. The heat in his eyes seemed banked by fear, giving credence to her assumption that his proposal was prompted by something other than romantic notions. The victory felt hollow.

"You know I love you, Bianca."

Her eyebrows shot up even as her heart plummeted. He loved her like a sister, had mentioned that often when he teased about needing to soak his feet in chilled water after helping her learn to dance. That he use such a phrase when he knew she meant something different hurt.

"Then kiss me." It was hard to tell who was more stunned by her challenge. It felt right, though. There was no better way to call him on his manipulation.

Landon looked awkward as he reached a shaky hand toward her cheek. He gently brushed the curls back, laying his hand along the side of her neck.

Her heartbeat increased. Was he going to take her challenge? Was it possible he felt more than she realized?

Ever so slowly, he leaned forward, bending his head toward hers. Their breath mingled, his spicy scent filling Bianca's senses until air backed up in her lungs. Her eyes drifted shut of their own volition, despite her desire to see every emotion in Landon's eyes.

His lips connected with hers in the softest caress imaginable, like a butterfly floating by. She waited for more, for him to sweep by again with a firmer pressure, to send her heart fluttering again, but it never came.

Then his hand was gone, leaving her neck cold. By the time she forced her eyes open, there was nothing to see but Landon's back as he fled down the stairs.

Landon paced his study from door to bookcase, seven long strides eating up the floor before he turned and did it again.

His staff was beginning to gather outside the door, occasionally sending someone to peek in on him and ask if he needed anything. They were beginning to look worried. Not that he blamed them. He'd been pacing since he fled here from Bianca's house hours ago.

This morning it had seemed so simple. He had gone to Bianca's house, determined to help her work out a plan for escaping Theodore. He'd had no intention of proposing she marry him. Had he?

As soon as he'd made the suggestion, he knew it was the right solution, the only solution. He was a viscount, outranking Theodore's potential barony. Not to mention he was a friend of the family and more of a gentleman than Theodore ever pretended to be. If she was looking for a practical match, he was a much better choice.

So why had she turned him down?

He changed direction and strode to the window, bracing his hands on either side. His reflection wavered in the glass as evening crept in. The face was one he'd seen every day of his life, but he didn't know the man anymore.

Since the first inklings of manhood he'd prided himself on keeping his eyes on God instead of the women that distracted so many of his friends. He'd called them fools, knowing that God would provide the right woman in time. Had he been too focused? Like a horse with blinders, so set on moving forward that he missed his destination?

Because he never expected the thought of kissing little Bianca Caulfield to shake him to his very core.

The kiss had been fleeting. He wasn't positive his lips had even touched hers, but from the first mention of marriage to the moment he'd rested his hand on her cheek, everything he knew about his life had crumbled in on itself. He'd never felt so out of control.

So why did the thought of putting everything back the way it had been tie his stomach in knots?

Even considering what he would need to do to put their relationship back on a friendly level sent panic to his toes.

He looked past his reflection to a couple walking down the street below his window. Their heads tilted towards each other in a sign of intimacy despite the proper amount of space between their strolling bodies. They were obviously in love.

Love.

Panic flowed from him like water. He loved Bianca. And not in the family way he'd always teased her about. Somewhere along the line as she'd grown into womanhood she'd made her way into his heart while she lowered her hemlines and put up her hair.

"George!" he bellowed.

The butler was instantly at the door. How many people were lingering out there? Why did he even care?

"My horse. Now."

Fifteen minutes later, he found himself in front of Bianca's house again, determination of a new kind driving him to knock with more force than necessary.

The door unlatched and Landon pushed his way in even as the butler opened it. "Where is she?"

"My lord!"

"Bianca – Miss Caulfield – where is she?"

"The drawing room, my lord, but I must protest –"

Whatever else the man said was lost as Landon's long legs ate up the floor to the drawing room he'd earlier made a fool of himself in.

There she was. Pretty as a painting with her blonde hair in a simple braid wrapped around her head, still in a plain afternoon dress. His heart threatened to beat its way out of his chest, but a sense of rightness that filled his soul made everything right. Brought peace to his soul.

Her bright blue eyes widened as she rose to her feet. "Landon?"

He didn't know how he crossed the room. He could have walked, run, or flew for all he knew and he truly didn't care, because whatever he'd done had brought her within reach. He leaned in even as he wrapped his arms around her, pulling her into his chest, his heart, where she belonged.

There was nothing hesitant about his kiss this time. The press of his lips to hers felt like coming home. Her fingers dove into his hair and she sighed into his kiss, relaxing into his arms.

He pulled back, but only far enough to see into her eyes. He rested his forehead against hers, fighting to steady his breath enough to speak. This precious girl, no, this precious woman had always been there for him. He couldn't imagine his life without her in it.

"I love you, Bianca."

She bit her lip. "Why now? You didn't this morning."

He smoothed the curls back from her face with a smile. "I think I did. I was just too thick to know it. You've always been part of my life, Bianca. I couldn't imagine building a life, having children, growing old with anyone else by my side. You are my beloved, my darling. Please tell me you'll be my bride."

Her eyes glistened with tears as a wide smile stretched across her face. She nodded, her hair rubbing against his forehead like silk. A light laugh escaped her lips even as a tear ran down her cheek. "Yes, my love. I'll be your bride."

Landon picked her up and spun her around, spying Giles leaning in the doorway.

With a bit of heat in his cheeks, Landon placed Bianca back on the floor but kept her close to his side.

"Finally," Giles said with a smile. "Welcome to the family."

Surprise caused Landon to go a bit slack-jawed. Giles had known? How could the man know something Landon hadn't even realized about himself?

He looked down at Bianca with her bright smile and loving eyes, and decided he didn't care. All that mattered was his own eyes had been opened before it was too late.

And they were going to live happily ever after.

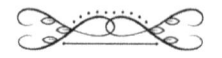

Three o'Clock in Portman Square

Three o'Clock in Portman Square

Royal Academy Art Exhibit, London, 1819

He'd painted her.

Miss Lydia Buchanan stood amongst the painting covered walls of the Royal Academy Exhibition and lifted her fingers to lightly trace the clover-shaped birthmark behind her right ear. Despite the shared coloring and the fact that she owned the same dress, Lydia wouldn't have believed the graceful goddess in the painting was meant to be her without the birthmark.

Was that how he saw her? Did he think her a woman with enough confidence and daring to dance through a garden alone? With enough grace to dance at all?

"What are you doing in the corner?" Lydia's sister, Jane, whispered in her ear. "I thought you were going to look for William Brussle's painting."

The way Jane dragged out the man's name in a breathy sigh made Lydia cringe. It had been foolish and try to hide her feelings for the painter from her family, particularly her sister. They'd been bound to notice that she found a reason to wander next door nearly every day.

Or at least she had before she'd ruined everything.

She'd wanted so badly for William to notice her, to see her as different from the many girls who hovered around his workspace, drawn by his looks and awed by his talent.

He certainly wasn't likely to forget her now. Tripping and spilling paint across the original picture he'd worked so hard to perfect for this exhibit was memorable in the worst of ways.

"I had planned to look for his work, yes," Lydia said, her voice quiet with confusion.

She couldn't forget his look of dismay as he'd tried to save his work - the dark frown of agony when he'd realized it was a futile effort. The memory had overtaken every charming smile she'd stored away until she could barely remember what he looked like happy. That he'd ever been happy.

Why paint her in such a flattering way after she'd ruined his work?

Jane scoffed. "You won't find him up in the corner. Brussle's much too good a painter to be skyed. I'm going to look at the sculptures."

Lydia murmured agreement, but she didn't follow.

Instead, her gaze stayed fixed on the painting on the top row, angled out from the wall, and shadowed from the glass roof. It was a humiliating position for the work of a man like him. His reputation and skill demanded that his work be displayed at eye level in the center of the wall.

Instead he'd been skyed, positioned near the ceiling with the lesser skilled painters, and it was all her fault.

Maybe it wasn't his. Maybe someone else had painted a woman with a startling resemblance to Lydia. Maybe...

She scrambled for the guidebook, flipping through the pages to the appropriate listing.

Three O'Clock in Portman Square by William Brussle.

The name didn't make sense, but the painting was most definitely his. There'd been his customary attention to detail, the swirl of the skirt around the dancing woman, the curls drifting about the face as if they were floating above the canvas. The rest of the painting was unremarkable, as if it had been done in a rush.

And it would have been. There'd been a mere three weeks between Lydia's display of remarkable clumsiness and the opening of the exhibit.

But why not submit one of his other paintings?

Why paint her of all people? She'd ruined the most beautiful painting she'd ever seen and he'd... rewarded her?

Her family circled the gallery and returned to her side. Her mother touched her shoulder. "Have you seen everything, dear?"

"Have you even left this spot?" Jane asked with a laugh. "Are you deciphering a hidden message in the paintings?"

Lydia blinked at her younger sister. A hidden message? Her gaze dropped back down to the pamphlet. It wasn't possible. Was it? Did he mean for her to see this painting? Was it a message meant for her?

With one last look at the painting, and one last longing that she could actually be the woman depicted there, Lydia allowed her family to lead her from the gallery.

Once home, they scattered to various afternoon amusements. Lydia paused in the act of removing her bonnet as the clock in the drawing room chimed.

One. Two. Three.

Three O'Clock in Portman Square.

The park was right outside her door. She could slip out of the house, ensure herself that the name and painting had merely been a coincidence, and be back home before anyone knew she'd even left.

Resolutely she retied her bonnet ribbons and slipped out the front door.

As she approached the gate, her breath grew harsher and faster than the short walk required. But it was nothing compared to the way her heart shuddered when she saw him there.

William leaned against a tree in the center of the park, head rested back against the trunk, allowing his brown curls to tangle in the rough bark, eyes closed.

"You painted me." Lydia said softly.

His head snapped up and his deep brown eyes opened. For several moments he simply stared at her.

"I had to," he said as he pushed away from the tree and took her limp hand in his. "You stopped coming. I couldn't imagine my studio without you, so I painted you there."

"But," she swallowed, "I ruined your painting."

He winced and looked down at their joined hands. "That you did." His eyes traveled slowly back up to hers. "But without you everything else is ruined."

His grip tightened around her fingers. "Be in my life, Lydia. Let me court you."

She couldn't have held back the smile or her tears of happiness, even if she'd wanted to. And looking better than any painting ever created, he smiled back.

The Heir Next Door

The Heir Next Door

With an unfortunate name like Florentia Frances Fernmore, she should have expected life had more than a few unpleasant surprises in store for her, but somehow she still thought that one day she would marry the man she fell in love with as a child.

Somewhere along the way the boy she'd been enamored with had become a man she didn't know. For years she'd been bringing a mid-day meal to her father's office where he worked as an estate manager for Lord Nordrum. Whenever Philip had been home on school break, she'd carefully timed her deliveries so that she would encounter him somewhere along the way.

If that meant occasionally lurking in the woods for an hour or so in order to approach the house when he was walking up from the stable, so be it. Of course, that meant her father's meal was occasionally delivered cold, but that dilemma was easily solved by packing a meal of cold meat and cheese whenever waiting might be a necessity.

Avoiding Philip's older brother Jasper was not quite as easily accomplished. Somehow he always knew where she was hiding or which route she had chosen.

More than once, he'd interrupted her asking Philip about school or London or his future plans.

More than once he'd come up behind her and asked if she needed assistance finding the way across the lawn to the house.

More than once she'd thought about kicking him in the shin to see if a flash of pain would wipe that arrogant frown from his face. Just because he would one day be the Earl of Nordrum didn't mean he had the right to interfere in her life.

At this moment, though, she wished someone would interfere in it. Some sort of benevolent godmother would make her day much brighter because at one-and-twenty, she wasn't getting any younger and all the dreams she'd once had for her life were now splattered in the dirt along with her father's roast beef.

She'd known Philip was due to arrive for a visit today and she'd dressed in her very best dress, determined that this time he would see that she would be the perfect choice of wife for a younger son intending to go into the church. It would seem, though, that Philip had already decided the daughter of a gentleman in Kent would make a better choice.

She couldn't fault him. From Florentia's vantage point amongst the shrubs at the corner of the house, the other woman appeared the very picture of quiet, humble sophistication.

The fine weather meant she was gaining abundance of dream-crushing information. Jasper had greeted his brother on the drive itself and enjoyed a prolonged conversation in the warm sunshine before taking the two inside to meet the earl and countess.

What was Florentia supposed to do now? There wasn't a great deal of demand for the daughters of estate managers in their small local society, and it wasn't as if Florentia could afford to travel somewhere and have any sort of season. Without Philip, her options consisted of being a shopkeeper's wife or taking a job herself as a governess or a companion.

She would have to stop coming to Ellwood Park, the only place that had ever truly felt like home. Even when she had to finagle her way through Jasper's derision, she breathed easier at Ellwood.

She ran a hand along the smooth granite corner of the building. She didn't have time to find a new dream. It was time to form a practical life. It was time to say goodbye.

Tears welled in her eyes and dripped over the ends of her lashes, blurring her vision as she abandoned the dropped plate of food and started across the lawn to return home.

"Leaving so soon?"

Florentia's head snapped up and she brushed quickly at her cheeks, recognizing Jasper's stern voice. There was no point in denying that she'd been listening in, no reason to pretend she hadn't heard.

She sniffled and sighed. "Yes, I'm leaving. I... Well, I think we both know why." She cast a longing look up the side of the house. "I'll miss this place."

Jasper coughed and shifted his position to keep her trapped amongst the shrubbery. "This place?"

His quizzical look speared through her and she ducked her head in hopes of hiding her suddenly warm cheeks. Once more she'd given Jasper reason to believe she was no more responsible than the little nine-year-old girl in braids that had climbed the tree to tap on Philip's window and ask if he wanted to go fishing.

Of course, she hadn't even been able to do that right since she had ended up tapping on Jasper's window. He'd been seventeen at the time and had made it a point to witness every one of her embarrassing moments ever since.

Including this one.

She nodded. "I've always liked it here."

"Your father still works here."

"Yes."

"You can still bring him food." He gave a wry grin. "Perhaps even hot food if you aren't preoccupied."

"Yes," she said quietly. "That would certainly free up some of your time."

"I've often thought of how I'd fill my time if you weren't chasing Philip."

The heat in her cheeks intensified and tears rushed into her eyes once more, fuller and heavier than they had before. What was wrong with her that the idea of no longer seeing Jasper made her cry even harder than Philip's looming betrothal? Why did his dreaming of the day she would let him be hurt worse than the loss of her childhood fantasies?

Shaking her head, she pushed past Jasper and ran across the lawn toward her small home on the edge of the property. She burst through the door, ignored the curious squeals of the servants, and locked herself in her room.

Not ten minutes later, a tapping sound drew her attention to the window.

Jasper was leaning against the glass.

She pushed open the sash. "Did I leave something behind?"

"I was wondering if you might like to go fishing."

Then he kissed her.

And it seemed there might actually be time for Florentia Frances Fernmore to find a new dream after all.

Also Available

Continue the story in The Haven Manor Series

A Defense of Honor
When Katherine "Kit" FitzGilbert turned her back on London society more than a decade ago, she determined never to set foot in a ballroom again. But when business takes her to London and she's forced to run for her life, she stumbles upon not only a glamorous ballroom but also Graham, Lord Wharton. What should have been a chance encounter becomes much more as Graham embarks on a search for his friend's missing sister and is convinced Kit knows more about the girl than she's telling.

After meeting Graham, Kit finds herself wishing things could have been different for the first time in her life, but what she wants can't matter. Long ago, she dedicated herself to helping women escape the same scorn that drove her from London and raising the innocent children caught in the crossfire. And as much as she desperately wishes to tell Graham everything, revealing the truth may come at too high a price for those she loves.

A Return of Devotion
Daphne Blakemoor was perfectly happy living in her own secluded world for twelve years. She had everything she needed—loved ones, a true home, and time to indulge her imagination. But when ownership of the estate where she works as a housekeeper passes on, and the new marquis has an undeniable connection to her past, everything she's come to rely upon is threatened.

William, Marquis of Chemsford's main goal in life is to be the exact opposite of his father. Starting a new life in the peace and quiet of the country sounds perfect until his housekeeper turns his life upside down.

A Pursuit of Home
In early 1800s England, Jess Beauchene has spent most of her life in hiding and always on the move in an effort to leave her past far behind her. But when she learns the family she thought had died just might be alive and in danger, she knows her secrets can only stay buried for so long.

Derek Thornbury loves the past, which has led him to become an expert in history and artifacts. He knows Jess has never liked him, but when she requests his help deciphering the clues laid out in an old family diary, he can't resist the urge to solve the puzzle.

As Jess and Derek race to find the hidden artifact before her family's enemies, they learn as much about each other as they do about the past. But can their search to uncover the truth of the past lead to a future together?

Learn about the latest releases, deals, and more by signing up for Kristi's newsletter at KristiAnnHunter.com.

Milton Keynes UK
Ingram Content Group UK Ltd.
UKHW011049201123
432908UK00006BA/830